I0526910

ANGEL WITH A
DIRTY FACE

JAMES SU

ANGEL WITH A DIRTY FACE
Copyright © 2025 by James Su
All rights reserved.

Front and back cover design by James Su

Written and printed in the U.S.A.

No part of this book may be copied, reproduced, distributed, or transmitted in any form or by any means, including photocopying, recording, or other electronic or mechanical methods, without the prior written permission of the author, except for brief quotations in a review.

This is a work of fiction. Any resemblance to actual persons, living or dead, or real-life events is purely coincidental.

Published by Cinehenge

www.cinehenge.com

First Edition: May, 2025

ISBN: 979-8-99874570-6

"A tiger's skin is easy to draw, but its bones are hard to depict; one can know a person's face, but not their heart."

—Chinese Proverb

PROLOGUE

The City of Angels at night was a contradiction. From the hills, it was breathtaking—a sprawling constellation of golden lights, the skyline shimmering against the dark, whispering promises of fortune, reinvention, and dreams fulfilled. The freeways slithered through the city like molten rivers of red and white, brake lights blinking like embers in the endless rush.

But up close, it was something else entirely: a labyrinth of excess, decay, superficiality, and danger where people clawed at each other for pieces of a dream that wasn't big enough for everyone.

On the quiet streets of the affluent area of Trousdale, away from the chaotic pulse of downtown, the city's edges were gone. Here, the streets were lined with manicured hedges and magnificent homes either tucked behind wrought-iron gates or arborvitae trees, their windows glowing softly in the dark. This was where the winners of Los Angeles' cruel game resided, shutting out the noise and chaos in favor of curated perfection. And among these homes stood the house of Danny and Lina (LEE-Nah) Carter—a sleek modern estate with floor-to-ceiling glass walls that framed their carefully constructed lives like an art installation.

But tonight, the Carter house was quiet. Too quiet.

Lina, mid-thirties, gorgeous, exudes sultry elegance—dark, wavy hair, almond-shaped brown eyes, and sculpted cheekbones. Shapely and polished, she moves with deliberate grace, a trophy wife who looks like a million bucks. She swirled the last of her chardonnay in the glass, staring at the glow of her phone screen as her friends' smiling faces filled the frame. Vanessa's pool party had been perfect: sunny skies, warm winter in the low seventies, bottomless mimosas, and endless compliments about her new dress.

It was the life Lina had always dreamed of—effortless, glamorous, and untouchable. But the quiet of the house felt heavier tonight, oppressive even. Danny was late, and she couldn't shake the feeling that something was off.

The front door opened suddenly, slamming against the wall, and she jumped, spilling a splash of wine onto her hand. She frowned, annoyed at first, but when she saw Danny step into the room, the irritation faded. His tie was loose, his suit jacket rumpled, and his face was pale and strained. His usual confidence—the calm, sharp control he carried into every room—was gone.

"Danny?" she asked, setting her glass on the counter. "What's wrong?" He didn't answer, moving past her to the liquor cabinet. The clink of the scotch bottle against the glass was sharp, grating. He poured himself a double, downed half in one swallow, and leaned heavily against the counter.

"Danny," she said again, her voice sharper this time. "You're scaring me. What happened? What's going on?"

"They're about to find out," he said flatly, staring into his drink.

"What? Find out about what?" she asked, stepping closer.

"My partners," he said, his tone cold and distant. "They're about to discover the embezzlement." The word hit her like a punch to the gut.

She froze, staring at him. "Embezzlement?" What the hell are you talking about?!"

He finally looked at her, his dark eyes hard and unyielding. "Do you really believe that I've been working sixty-hour weeks for a six-figure salary? No, Lina. I've been skimming off the top for years. Millions. And now they're about to figure it out."

Lina's stomach churned. "You've been stealing millions?!" she whispered. Danny set the glass down with a sharp clink, his jaw tight.

"Don't act so surprised. You've been spending that money without a second thought. You didn't ask where it came from because you didn't want to know. Don't pretend you're innocent in this."

Her breath hitched, and something inside her snapped.

"Are you kidding me?" she yelled, her voice rising. "You've been lying to me this whole time? You put our lives at risk, and you didn't think I deserved to know?"

Danny flinched as she stormed toward him, her hands balled into fists. She pounded on his chest and shoulders, her blows weak but frantic. "How could you do this, Danny? How could you lie to me like this? Everything we've built— everything I thought we had—it's all a lie!"

"Lina—" he began, but she didn't stop. She hit him again, harder this time, until her knees gave out, and she crumpled to the floor. The sobs came immediately, violently, shaking her shoulders as she buried her face in her hands. Danny stared down at her, his expression unreadable. After a moment, he crouched beside her and grabbed her by the shoulders, forcing her to look at him. His voice was calm, measured, but there was an edge of urgency beneath it.

"Listen to me, Lina. Listen! I've been preparing for this. I knew it was only a matter of time before they caught on, and I've got a plan—a perfect plan. But we need to move fast."

She shook her head, her tears streaking her cheeks. "I can't... I can't do this, Danny. I can't throw away everything like this."

He gripped her shoulders tighter, his tone softening but losing none of its intensity. "You think I'd let this happen without a way out? I've been setting this up for years. We'll disappear, and no one will ever find us. But we have to act now."

4

Lina blinked at him, her breaths shallow and uneven. "Now? You're telling me all of this now, and you expect me to just... go along with it?"

"I don't have a choice," Danny said. "And neither do you. If we don't move quickly, they'll come after me—and you. They'll freeze the accounts and seize everything. Do you understand what that means? Everything will be gone, all of it. We'll walk out of here in handcuffs."

Her lips trembled as she stared at him, her mind racing. The thought of losing it all—the life as she knew it and had grown so accustomed to, the comfort, the money, the lifestyle, the security—was unfathomable and unbearable. "How long do we have?" she whispered.

"I can stall them for a couple of months," Danny said, releasing her shoulders and standing. He began to pace the room, his movements sharp and restless. "The whole computer system is gonna be upgraded at the firm. They're gonna implement AI into the system. It's gonna take a little while, but when it's done, the embezzlement will surely surface. We need to execute the plan now. Every second we waste is another second closer to everything falling apart."

Lina wiped at her face, trying to steady her breathing. Her heart felt like it was tearing itself apart, caught between the life she knew and the unknown future Danny was offering. "And if I say no?"

Danny stopped pacing and turned to face her, his expression hard. "I already told you, you don't get to say no.

5

You're in this whether you like it or not. That money you've been spending? It's dirty. They'll think you're a part of it. We both go down."

Her stomach twisted, and she felt a fresh wave of tears welling up. "You bastard," she whispered. "You've trapped me."

"No," he said firmly, stepping closer. "I've given you a way out. You just have to trust me."

Lina stared at him, her mind reeling. She didn't trust him—not anymore. But what choice did she have? She didn't know any life other than the one she had now. Without Danny, without his money, she would be nothing. "Fine," she said finally, her voice barely audible. "Tell me what to do."

Danny's lips curved into a small, satisfied smile. "Good. We'll go over the details. For now, just follow my lead." Lina nodded feebly, but inside, a storm was raging.

She had no idea what she was agreeing to, no idea how her life was about to change. But one thing was certain: nothing would ever be the same again.

The house was silent. Too silent. Lina sat at the edge of the bed, still in her silk robe, her bare feet touching the cool hardwood floor.

The morning light streamed in through the tall windows, soft and golden, painting the room in a warmth that felt utterly cold from the knot of dread in her stomach. She had barely slept. Her mind had been spinning all night, replaying Danny's words over and over until they blurred into a dull, suffocating hum.

They're about to find out.

I have a plan.

You're in this whether you like it or not.

We both go down.

She pressed her hands to her face, trying to steady her breathing. When she finally stood, her knees felt weak, her body sluggish as if it were weighed down by the enormity of it all. Danny had already left for work, as if it were just another normal day. But nothing about this day was normal. It was the day after her life had been turned upside down.

Lina wandered out of the bedroom and into the hallway, her hand trailing along the polished bannister as she descended the staircase. Her fingers trembled slightly, and she clenched them into a fist, forcing herself to keep moving.

She stepped into the living room, pausing in the center of the space, and let her eyes roam over everything she and Danny had built—or what she *thought* they had built.

The leather sectional couch, sleek and modern, had been Danny's pick, but she had chosen the throw pillows—cream and navy blue, with subtle geometric patterns.

She had spent hours arranging them just so, making sure the space looked elegant but lived-in, like the kind of home people envied when they came over for wine and hors d'oeuvres.

Her gaze drifted to the fireplace mantel, where a collection of framed photos stood in neat rows. She stepped closer, picking one up—a picture from their honeymoon in Fiji.

She had her arms wrapped around Danny's neck, her head tilted back in laughter as the sun set behind them.

She remembered that moment vividly: the taste of the crisp white wine, the warmth of Danny's hand on her waist. She had been so happy. Or maybe she had just been naïve. She placed the photo back carefully, her fingers lingering on the edge of the frame before moving on.

In the dining room, sunlight glinted off the glass table, making it sparkle. She ran her hand over its surface, her fingertips brushing against the crystal vase in the center. It was filled with fresh lilies—her favorite. Danny had brought them home two days ago, casually setting them on the counter as if it were an afterthought. She had been touched at the time. Now, the gesture felt hollow, like a magician's sleight of hand meant to distract her from what was really happening.

Her chest tightened as she moved into the kitchen. This was her sanctuary, the place where she hosted brunches and prepared charcuterie boards that always got compliments. The marble countertops gleamed, spotless as ever, and the copper pots hanging above the island caught the light, their warm glow a stark contrast to the chill that crept up her spine.

She reached out and touched the largest pot, her hand quivering as she remembered the countless meals she had made here—the pasta nights, the roasted vegetables, the delicate pastries she had taught herself to bake during lockdown.

All of it would be gone soon. Lina stepped through the French doors and onto the patio, the cool morning air brushing against her cheeks. The yard stretched out before her, immaculate and vibrant. The rose bushes along the fence were in full bloom, their deep red petals glistening with dew.

She had spent so much time here, pruning the flowers, arranging bouquets for the dining table, sipping coffee in the mornings as she listened to the birds. It was her favorite part of the house, her retreat from the chaos of the world. She bent down and cupped a single bloom in her hand, inhaling its delicate fragrance as tears welled up in her eyes.

"Goodbye," she whispered, her voice breaking. "Goodbye, my beautiful life." Her knees felt weak again, and she sank onto the edge of the patio steps, her hands trembling in her lap. The tears came then, slow and silent, tracing warm paths down her cheeks. She wiped them away quickly, as if denying them would make this nightmare less real. But it *was* real. The life she had curated so carefully—the parties, the friends, the comfort—was crumbling beneath her, and there was nothing she could do to stop it. She wrapped her arms around herself, shivering despite the sun's warmth. Danny's plan would take everything from her. Everything except him.

Her gaze drifted back toward the house, her eyes lingering on the sleek lines of the roof, the pristine white walls, the windows that sparkled like diamonds in the morning light. This house had been her stage, her sanctuary, her fortress. And soon, it would be nothing more than a memory.

Lina stood slowly, brushing the dirt from her robe, and turned back toward the doors. Her reflection stared back at her in the glass—disheveled, hollow, a ghost of the woman she had been just yesterday. She placed her hand on the door handle, her fingers tightening around the cool metal. "Get it together," she murmured to herself, her voice steadying. "You're stronger than this." With one last glance at the yard, she stepped inside and closed the door behind her.

The quiet of the house enveloped her once more, and for a moment, she just stood there, letting the silence settle over her like a heavy blanket. And then, with a deep breath, she moved toward the stairs. There were things to pack, plans to make. If this life was ending, she would face it on her own terms.

1. THE FIRST RIDE

The City of Angels bled neon. It sprawled beneath a veil of artificial light, pulsing and shifting, like it had a heartbeat of its own.

This is February, the streets shimmered, their surfaces slick with the remnants of an earlier rain, reflecting the reds, greens, and yellows of traffic lights in a kaleidoscope of motion. Horns blared in frustration, engines hummed like restless bees, and the occasional screech of brakes cut through the night.

Leslie Lai's 2020 Toyota Prius weaved through the chaos, a lone vessel in an ocean of urban turmoil. Inside, the air was stale with a faint hint of cheap air freshener—"New Car Scent," though the car hadn't felt new in years. Leslie, 33, lean with sharp cheekbones, disheveled black hair, and shadowed eyes. Nondescript features, the kind of face people forgot the second they walked away. His eyes were bloodshot from a lack of sleep, and the wrinkled button-up he wore spoke of effort— just not enough.

His slumped posture and frayed clothing reflect a quiet sadness, blending into the world he resents. The faint blue glow of his dashboard lit up his tired face, the Uber app blinking: **"SEARCHING FOR PASSENGER."**

He adjusted his grip on the steering wheel, his knuckles brushing against the cracked faux leather cover. His shoulders slouched, and his posture bore the weight of too many hours spent behind the wheel.

His reflection in the rearview mirror looked back at him: unremarkable, weary, and vaguely detached

Being a rideshare driver taught him one thing: people were the worst.

He scrolled through a playlist on his phone, flicking past tracks with a sigh. One uninspired pop song after another, each one somehow grating yet forgettable.

Finally, he selected one at random, letting the melody wash over him like white noise. His gaze shifted to the road ahead, his expression detached. He'd driven them all: the drunks, the cheaters, the liars, the Karens. Each ride was like a front-row seat to the slow, inevitable collapse of humanity. The memories surfaced unbidden, a montage of late-night encounters he'd rather forget.

A young man stumbled out of a nightclub, his designer jacket draped over one arm like a trophy of his poor decisions. He collapsed into Leslie's back seat, the smell of tequila thick in the air. "Bro, take me to... hic... In-N-Out," he slurred, fumbling with his seatbelt. "You're paying, right? Hero, man." His head lolled against the window as Leslie glanced at him in the rearview mirror, unimpressed.

Some just wanted a babysitter.

The dashboard clock blinked 11:47 PM in pale green light as Leslie's Prius crept through the streets of Los Angeles. The city was alive, but not in the way people romanticized it.

It wasn't the L.A. of sunshine and palm trees, of dreams fulfilled and celebrities strolling hand-in-hand down Rodeo Drive. No, this was a city of neon grime, of broken lives held together with booze and bravado. The kind of city where dreams didn't come true—they came to die.

Leslie tapped his fingers against the steering wheel, his hand hovering over the app as another ride request pinged through. He sighed and accepted it, even though his back ached and his eyes burned from staring at brake lights for hours. *Just a couple more rides,* he told himself. But he knew better. He'd keep driving until exhaustion made his limbs feel like lead, because there was nothing else waiting for him when he got home. No one.

The address popped up: a trendy rooftop bar in West Hollywood. Leslie already knew the type of person he'd be picking up—some influencer or tech bro too drunk to realize that the world didn't revolve around their every whim. He pulled up to the curb, engine idling, and waited.

She stumbled out first. Tall, tan, blonde—straight out of some reality TV show casting call. She wore a tiny sequined dress that glittered under the streetlights, but it wasn't enough to distract from the mess of mascara smeared beneath her eyes. Her

13

phone was glued to her hand, the screen casting a ghostly glow on her face. A guy followed her, equally drunk but louder, his voice cutting through the night like a blade. "Get in the car!" she snapped, fumbling with the door handle before collapsing into the backseat. The guy laughed and took his time lighting a cigarette even as Leslie stared at him through the rearview mirror. He hated when they smoked near his car—the stink clung to the seats no matter how much Glade he sprayed.

"Can you, uh, not smoke by the car?" Leslie said, his voice even but tired.

The guy rolled his eyes, tossing the cigarette onto the sidewalk with a showy flick. "Relax, man."

Leslie bit his tongue and looked straight ahead. It wasn't worth it. They fell into the backseat in a tangle of limbs, too busy yelling at each other to notice him. She was scrolling through Instagram, her fingers swiping furiously as if the answers to her problems were buried in the filtered lives of strangers. He was muttering about how she was "embarrassing him in front of his boys." They barely acknowledged Leslie's existence, as if he were a piece of furniture with wheels.

"Where are we headed?" Leslie asked after a moment, keeping his tone neutral. He had learned long ago not to sound too interested. Drunk people liked to talk if you gave them an opening, and he had no desire to hear whatever sob story they thought was important. "Home," she slurred, waving her phone at him. "I already put the address in. Just—drive." The address was in Beverly Hills. Of course it was.

The streets blurred past in streaks of light and shadow as Leslie drove, his hands gripping the wheel tighter than necessary.

In the backseat, their argument escalated. He could hear every word, though he tried to tune it out.

"You're such a child," she hissed. "Do you even care about me at all?" "Don't start with this again, Jen" the guy shot back. "You're acting crazy."

Leslie's jaw clenched. The words sounded familiar, painfully so.

For a moment, he was back in that kitchen with Rachel, her voice breaking as she told him she couldn't do it anymore. That she couldn't keep loving someone who didn't love themselves. He blinked hard, forcing the memory away.

"You're pathetic," the woman said, her voice cracking. "Just leave. Go back to your boys. Go back to whoever you were flirting with at the bar." The guy leaned forward, jabbing his finger at her. "You're the one who started this! You're the one who's—"

"Hey!" Leslie snapped, his voice cutting through the chaos. They both went silent, startled. For the first time, they looked at him, really looked at him. "Keep it down," Leslie said, his tone sharp but even. "Or I'll pull over and you can walk the rest of the way."

The guy scoffed, leaning back in his seat. "Whatever, man."

Leslie didn't reply. He just kept driving, his knuckles white against the wheel.

When he finally pulled up to their address, neither of them said thank you. The guy threw the door open and stumbled out, while the woman lingered for a moment, staring at her phone as if debating whether to call someone. She finally slid out of the car without a word, her sequined dress catching the light one last time before she disappeared into the night.

Leslie watched them go, his chest heavy with something he couldn't quite name. He tapped "Ride Completed" on the app and stared at the glowing screen for a moment, the silence of the car pressing in around him.

People call Los Angeles a city of angels, but all he ever saw were ghosts and devils—restless, desperate souls drifting through their lives, unaware of how close they were to falling apart.

Sometimes, he wondered if he was one of them. The next ride request buzzed through his phone. He accepted it without thinking.

The rain started somewhere near Santa Monica, light at first, then harder, fat drops streaking across Leslie's windshield as he idled outside a restaurant called Macciano's, the faint aroma of Italian cuisine wafting through the air. The glow of string lights framed the doorway, where a few patrons stood around under the green awning talking.

The APP had pinged him here five minutes ago, but whoever had requested the ride hadn't come out yet. Leslie hated

16

when people made him wait, but he didn't have it in him to cancel. It wasn't like he had anywhere better to be.

He glanced at the name on the APP. *Lina.* It was simple, elegant. Not like the usual drunken nicknames or fake monikers people used. Something about it stuck in his head. Just as he was about to tap his horn, the door to the restaurant opened, and she stepped out.

For a moment, Leslie forgot to breathe. What an angelic face!

She moved through the rain like it wasn't even there, her heels clicking softly against the wet pavement. A trench coat hung loosely from her shoulders, the belt untied and trailing behind her like a shadow.

Her dark hair clung to her face in damp strands, and her eyes—Leslie couldn't see the color from here, but they were sharp, cutting through the haze of the rain and streetlights. She held a small leather bag close to her chest, her movements precise, almost deliberate.

She wasn't beautiful in the way Hollywood churned out starlets. No, her stunning beauty was something else—raw, understated, the kind that could catch you off guard and leave you off balance. It wasn't just how she looked, though. It was the way she carried herself, like she belonged to another world entirely. Could she be an escort? Even if she was, he couldn't afford it.

Leslie sat up straight in his seat as she approached, suddenly aware of how his car smelled faintly of tequila from the last couple and the pine-scented air freshener dangling from the mirror. He reached for the window switch just as she leaned down to peer inside.

"You're Leslie?" Her voice was low, smooth, with the faintest edge of something—was it exhaustion? Or maybe disinterest? He couldn't tell, but it made him want to hear her speak again.

"Yeah," he said, his throat dry. He cleared it quickly and nodded toward the passenger door. "That's me. You can, uh, hop in."

She hesitated, her eyes flicking past him to the empty backseat. For a moment, he thought she might walk away, and a strange pang of disappointment tightened in his chest. But then she smiled—just barely, the corner of her mouth lifting as if she'd decided something—and opened the back passenger door.

The scent of her perfume rushed in the car as she settled into the backseat, a faint mix of something floral and smoky. It lingered in the air, clinging to the fabric of his seats like a whisper.

She crossed her legs, revealing a flash of smooth skin where her coat parted, and glanced at him in the mirror. "Thanks for waiting," she said softly, tucking her hair behind her ear. "I wasn't sure if you'd still be here."

"No problem," Leslie replied, forcing himself to sound casual, as if his heart wasn't pounding just a little faster.

"Trousdale?"

She was still settling in, making adjustment to her position in the seat. Her fingers tightened around the strap before she finally spoke. "Yes, please."

"You got it." Leslie replied quickly. It was one of those upscale neighborhoods that Leslie has driven to a few times. If he had to guess, this was either home or a "client's" place.

Leslie eased the car back into traffic, his hands gripping the wheel tighter than necessary. The rhythmic thud of the windshield wipers filled the silence, but his thoughts were louder. He found himself glancing at her in the rearview mirror more than he should, studying the sharp line of her jaw, the curve of her lips. She didn't look like the type of person who'd take an rideshare. She didn't look like the type of person who needed anyone's help at all.

"How's your evening so far?" he asked finally, the words slipping out before he could stop them.

She didn't answer right away. For a moment, he thought she might ignore him entirely. But then she turned her head, her eyes meeting his in the mirror.

"Rough night," she said, her lips curving into a wry smile. "But then again, every night's rough, isn't it?"

Leslie didn't know how to respond to that, so he didn't. Instead, he focused on the road, though his mind was anything but clear. She had a way of speaking that made everything sound heavier, like there were layers beneath her words that he wasn't meant to see.

19

He wondered what she was running from, what kind of storm had driven her out into the rain and into his car.

The ride has been quiet, but Leslie couldn't help but wanting to say something. Say anything. He is usually very good at talking to customers, but Lina, he couldn't come up with words. Finally, "that restaurant... Italian, right?"

She glanced at him in the mirror, her lips curving into the faintest hint of a smile. "Yes."

"Any good?"

"Very," she said, her voice softening just a little. "Especially Wednesday nights. You should try it."

Leslie chuckled. "Maybe I will."

"You're observant," she noted.

"About what?"

"The restaurant," she said. "Being Italian."

"The name gave it away," he replied with a grin.

For the first time, her smile widened slightly, though it didn't quite reach her eyes. "True. Pretty obvious."

They pulled up to a gated mansion that felt more like a fortress than a home. The manicured lawn, the glowing windows, the grand fountain—it all looked like something out of a magazine. Leslie parked the Prius, glancing at the towering gates. His car felt impossibly small here, a pebble in the shadow of a mountain.

Lina didn't move right away. She sat there, her hand resting lightly on the door handle, her gaze fixed on the gate of the house.

"Thanks for the ride," her voice soft.

She opened the door and stepped out into the rain without looking back. But just as Leslie was about to drive away, she leaned down and tapped on the window. He rolled it down, his pulse quickening.

"Here," she said, holding out a folded bill. "For waiting." Before he could refuse, she slipped it through the window and turned, walking into the haze of rain and the faint street light.

Leslie unfolded the bill as she entered the gate of the mansion. A twenty. He stared at it for a moment, then tucked it into his pocket, his mind racing.

He didn't know who she was or why she'd stuck with him the way she had. She could have just tipped him in the APP. In any case, that should've been the end of it, just another ride, another stranger, another forgettable moment. But it wasn't.

Not even close.

2. SOMETHING TO LOOK FORWARD TO

Leslie sprawled across the lumpy couch in his apartment, the muted drone of a late-night infomercial filling the silence. The salesman on the screen promised miracles in the form of a multi-bladed kitchen tool, his voice teeming with false enthusiasm. Leslie wasn't watching. His gaze drifted past the television to the blank wall beyond, his thoughts far from slicing and dicing.

A ping from his phone broke the monotony. He didn't need to look at the screen to know what it was—a new ride request. The familiar sound grated on him, a reminder that his life was dictated by strangers and their whims. He groaned, swiping the notification away without hesitation. For once, he didn't care if it affected his acceptance rate.

Instead, he opened the Uber app—not to work but to scroll aimlessly through his past rides. His finger hovered over the screen, his mind replaying the brief moments he'd shared with Lina. She had barely spoken during the drive, but somehow her silence had left an impression louder than any conversation.

She didn't belong in this city, he thought. In my car. In my life. And yet, out of all the rides in all of LA, she'd ended up in mine.

The memory of her lingered—her elegance, her sadness, the way she seemed to carry a weight she refused to share. It was more than infatuation; it was curiosity, a pull he couldn't explain. He wanted to see her again. No, he needed to.

Leslie sat up, his fingers drumming against his phone. He had an idea, one that teetered on the edge of rationality.

Maybe if he returned to the restaurant where he'd picked her up, he might see her again. It was a long shot, a gamble. But what did he have to lose? His life was already an endless loop. At least this would give him something to look forward to.

3. THE FARE REVISITED

The following Wednesday, Leslie parked his Prius outside Macciano's, his palms sweating against the steering wheel. It was a clear night. The street was bathed in golden light from the restaurant's string bulbs, their gentle glow dim the twinkles of the stars above. Patrons filtered in and out of the restaurant, laughter and snippets of conversation spilling into the night air.

He wasn't even sure what he was doing here. Maybe it was foolish—borderline obsessive—but part of him felt tonight was meant to be. The universe had handed him Lina once before. Maybe it would again.

His phone pinged.

He glanced at the screen, and his breath hitched. **Pickup request: Lina.**

Leslie's pulse quickened as he hit **Accept Ride.**

Moments later, the door to the restaurant swung open, and there she was.

Lina stepped out into the night, a vision in a sleek black dress. Her hair was pulled back elegantly, revealing her sharp

cheekbones and delicate neck. She looked different tonight—
more composed, more polished—but that air of sadness still
clung to her, a shadow she couldn't shake. She spotted his car
and walked toward him, her heels clicking softly against the
pavement. This time, there was no hesitation as she opened the
door and slid into the back seat.

"Hello again," he said, his voice careful.

She paused for a beat, her lips curling into a faint smile.
"Hello yourself. What a coincidence."

Leslie chuckled nervously, adjusting the rearview mirror
to meet her gaze. "Same address, that must be home."

"Actually," she said, her voice soft but steady, "can we
just drive for a bit? Maybe take the long way home?"

Leslie raised an eyebrow but nodded. "Well, I can't go
too far off the grid, but I could take the scenic route."

"That works," Lina replied, settling into her seat. "Do
what you need."

Leslie pulled away from the curb, the Prius humming as
it glided through the city streets. The silence between them was
heavy, but it wasn't uncomfortable. Lina gazed out the window,
her reflection flickering against the glass as the streetlights
passed.

"Have you ever felt... stuck?" she asked suddenly, her
voice cutting through the stillness.

Leslie frowned, glancing at her in the mirror. "What do
you mean?"

25

"Like your life is one endless loop," she said, her gaze still fixed on the window. "And no matter what you do, you can't break out of it."

Leslie let out a soft, bitter chuckle. "Yeah. I think you just described my life."

A faint smile tugged at the corners of Lina's lips, but it didn't reach her eyes. "Mine too," she murmured.

They stopped at a red light, and Leslie turned to look at her. There was something in her tone—a quiet despair—that made his chest tighten. "What's keeping you stuck?" he asked.

Lina hesitated, her fingers tracing invisible patterns on her lap. "It's complicated," she said finally.

Before Leslie could press further, the light turned green, and the moment passed.

The Prius came to a smooth stop in front of the mansion. Its grandeur was even more striking under the moonlight, the fountain in the driveway casting shimmering reflections on the stone façade. Lina lingered in her seat for a moment, her hand resting lightly on the door handle.

"Thank you, Leslie," she said, her voice softer than before.

Leslie blinked. It was the first time she'd said his name, and it sent an unexpected thrill through him. "Anytime," he replied.

Lina's fingers tightened slightly on the handle, but she didn't move. Instead, she glanced at him, her eyes searching his. "Maybe... I'll see you again?" she said, her tone uncertain.

"Yeah," Leslie said quickly, his heart thudding. "Maybe."

She smiled faintly and opened the door. Just as she stepped out, she turned back. "I'll be at the Vivid Night Club tomorrow," she said. "I should be done by midnight."

Leslie nodded, tried to be cool and masked the eagerness in his voice. "I'll try to be around."

She disappeared into the mansion, and Leslie sat there for a long moment, her scent—a mix of jasmine and something deeper—still lingering in the car. He inhaled and exhaled slowly, his hands gripping the wheel.

There was something about her.

He couldn't stop thinking about her, couldn't shake the feeling that she was pulling him into something far beyond a simple ride. He was in too deep, and he didn't even know it yet.

4. LAST RIDE OF THE NIGHT

The bass from Vivid Night Club pulsed through the street, a heartbeat that thudded in time with the chaos of Los Angeles nightlife. A kaleidoscope of lights spilled from the club's entrance, neon blues and purples mingling with the yellow-orange glow of streetlights. The air was thick with the scent of spilled drinks, late-night food trucks, and too much perfume.

Leslie sat in his Prius, parked just down the street, gripping the steering wheel with damp palms. He adjusted his shirt for the third time, tugging at the fabric as though that might somehow make it look less worn. His heart thumped unevenly, a rhythm out of sync with the club's music.

The doors of the nightclub swung open, and then he saw her.

Lina emerged, commanding attention without trying. Her fitted red strapless bustier dress with a front side slit shimmered faintly under the streetlights, hugging her in all the right places. Her hair was styled in 1940's retro, exposing the elegant curve of her neck. She paused on the sidewalk, scanning the row of idling cars with an air of quiet authority, as though she already knew who was waiting for her.

Her eyes landed on him.

Leslie straightened reflexively, running a hand over his face and wiping his palms against his jeans. His heart skipped as Lina approached, her heels clicking softly against the pavement. She opened the back door and slid in with effortless grace, the faint floral scent of her perfume immediately filling the car.

She tilted her head, a teasing smile playing on her lips. "We've got to stop meeting like this."

Leslie chuckled awkwardly, gripping the steering wheel. "Yeah, people might start to talk."

Her laughter was soft, almost musical, as she settled into the seat and crossed her legs with a fluid motion.

"Maybe I like running into you," she said, her gaze flicking to his in the rearview mirror.

He tried to hide the grin tugging at the corners of his mouth, focusing on the app instead. "Looks like we're headed to... Angel's Lounge?"

"It's a quiet place," she replied, brushing an invisible speck from her dress. "Good drinks. I thought we could talk."

His pulse quickened. "You mean... after the ride?"

She tilted her head, her smirk deepening. "I put in the destination for a reason."

Leslie hesitated for a moment, then swallowed hard and nodded. "Alright. Last ride of the night."

The Prius glided through quieter streets, the chaos of the nightclub fading behind them. The city lights became a blur, streaking past the windows like neon smudges on a canvas. Inside the car, the silence was thick but not oppressive. Lina gazed out at the city, her expression calm but distant.

"So, Leslie," she began, her voice breaking the quiet. "Why do you do rideshare?"

He tightened his grip on the wheel, his eyes fixed on the road ahead. "It pays the bills. Barely. And it's... simple."

"Simple doesn't seem like your style," she said, leaning back and studying him in the rearview mirror.

He laughed softly, shaking his head. "You don't know me well enough to say that."

"Maybe I'd like to," she replied, her tone light but laced with something deeper.

Leslie felt his throat tighten. He wanted to say something, anything, but the words wouldn't come.

5. ANGEL'S LOUNGE

Angel's Lounge was a far cry from the electric chaos of Vivid Nightclub. The bar sat tucked on a quiet corner, its understated exterior lit by a simple red neon sign that read **ANGEL'S** in looping script. The warm glow of hanging lights spilled through the windows, hinting at the cozy intimacy inside.

Leslie parked the Prius and turned off the engine, glancing nervously at Lina. "Here we are," he said.

She opened the door but paused, looking back at him with a raised eyebrow. "You're not just going to sit out here, are you?"

Leslie hesitated, his hands gripping the steering wheel. Then, with a deep breath, he unbuckled his seatbelt. "I guess one drink wouldn't hurt."

Her smile widened, and she stepped out, leading the way toward the bar.

Inside, the lounge was warm and inviting. Low music played in the background, blending with the quiet murmur of conversation. The amber glow of hanging lights bathed the room in a golden hue, reflecting off the polished wood of the bar and tables.

Lina and Leslie settled into a booth in the corner, away from the other patrons. She ordered a martini, her movements poised and deliberate, while Leslie opted for a beer, his nerves palpable.

"You always this quiet?" she asked, her eyes studying him over the rim of her glass.

He chuckled, shifting in his seat. "I'm just... not used to this."

"Used to what?"

"Talking to someone like you."

Her eyebrow arched, and a playful smirk tugged at her lips. "Someone like me?"

"You're... different," he said, the words tumbling out before he could stop them.

"Different can be good, you know," she said, swirling her drink.

The conversation ebbed and flowed, comfortable yet charged with unspoken tension. Finally, Lina leaned forward, her voice softening. "Leslie, do you believe in second chances?"

He frowned, caught off guard. "I guess so."

"Even for people who've made mistakes?"

"Everyone deserves a chance to make things right," he said slowly.

Her eyes glistened, her vulnerability flickering to the surface. "I've made a lot of mistakes."

"We all have," he replied.

Lina's hand brushed against his, her touch sending a jolt through him. "You're kind, Leslie," she said softly. "Not many people are."

Leslie swallowed hard, his pulse quickening as he stared at her. "I don't know about that."

She leaned in closer, her voice dropping to a whisper. "I do."

The air between them buzzed with unspoken energy as they sat in the corner of Angel's Lounge. Lina's eyes lingered on Leslie, their depths unreadable but compelling. He could feel the heat of her gaze, but it wasn't just her beauty that drew him in— it was the weight of something darker beneath the surface, a quiet storm she carried with her.

Leslie sipped his beer, trying to steady his nerves. His fingers fidgeted with the glass, the condensation cool against his palm. He'd never been good at moments like this, when everything felt charged and precarious. But with Lina, he didn't want to break the spell.

"You seem nervous," she said, tilting her head as she studied him.

He chuckled, shaking his head. "I'm not used to... attention."

"Attention?" she repeated, a faint smile tugging at her lips. "You mean someone noticing you?"

Leslie shrugged, his cheeks flushing. "Something like that."

Lina leaned forward, resting her chin lightly on her hand. "You're interesting, Leslie."

He laughed, a bitter edge to the sound. "I think you might be the first person to say that."

Her smile widened slightly, but her eyes remained serious. "You don't give yourself enough credit."

"Maybe," he admitted, lowering his gaze. He wasn't used to compliments. They felt foreign, like a language he didn't know how to speak.

The bartender passed by, setting Lina's second martini on the table. She took a slow sip, her red lipstick leaving a faint mark on the glass. "Tell me something about yourself," she said, her voice soft but insistent.

"Like what?"

"Anything. Something real."

Leslie hesitated, his fingers tracing the rim of his beer glass. "There's not much to tell. I drive. I live. That's about it."

She frowned, her brows knitting together. "That's not living, Leslie. That's surviving."

Her words hit him harder than he expected, and he looked up, meeting her gaze. For a moment, the noise of the bar faded, and it was just the two of them in the quiet, heavy space between truths.

"What about you?" he asked, his voice low. "What's your real story?"

Her smile faltered, and she leaned back, her expression guarded. "It's complicated."

"You keep saying that."

"Because it is." Her voice had a sharper edge now, but she softened it with a faint smile. "Maybe I'll tell you someday."

Leslie's quiet, he didn't want to push. Having drinks with a gorgeous and mysterious woman is something that he has never done before.

"Come on Leslie, let's get out of here."

She opened up her designer purse and pulled out a twenty-dollar bill. She set it on the table. Lina got up and so did Leslie. She led the way and they exited the lounge.

Lina turned her head back to Leslie and sent him a very devilish smile. Even though Leslie was not an experienced man, he knew that smile meant something. Lina kept walking towards Leslie's car and he admired her from behind -- the way she walked, the hair, her plump rear end, and those twelve-centimeter red bottom heels.

She reached his car and Leslie caught up. There was definitely sexual tension.

"Aren't you gonna unlock the door?" She said in a playful mood.

"Oh yes, sorry," Leslie fumbled through his pocket, pulled out his key fob, and pressed a button. The car beeped and unlocked. Lina opened the door and slid in.

"C'mon, sit with me here for a while."

Leslie knew she meant a different kind of "sitting." He got into the back seat with her and closed the door. As soon as the door closed, Lina mounted Leslie. This caught him off guard, but he didn't complain and went along with it.

She kissed him with passion and he reciprocated. They tore each other's clothes off. For the next heaven knew how long, there were two less lonely people in the world.

6. THE RIDE BACK

The drive back to Lina's mansion was quiet. The city, which had pulsed with life earlier, now seemed subdued, its streets bathed in the soft glow of streetlights. Leslie's Prius hummed along the pavement, the sound almost soothing.

Lina sat in the front passenger seat this time, her posture relaxed but her gaze distant. Her hair is a little messy, she did a passing job tidying up her hair after their vigorous exercise. She looked out the window, her expression enigmatic, as though she were seeing something far beyond the streets of Los Angeles.

Leslie gripped the wheel, sneaking glances at her out of the corner of his eye. The tension between them eased up a little, but feels like it could come back anytime. He wasn't sure what to say—if he should say anything at all. But the silence felt comfortable. It was more like a satisfying companionship and yet there seemed to be questions waiting to be answered.

"Have you ever done this before?" she asked suddenly, her tone teasing.

Leslie smiled, shaking his head. "No. You're the first."

She turned to look at him, her lips curving into a faint smile. "I will give you another stellar review."

"Sure, just leave out the steamy part. I might lose my job."

Lina laughs. This humor truly got her. They fell silent again, the car gliding through the quiet streets.

Leslie's mind raced, replaying their conversation at the bar, the way her hand had lingered on his, the vulnerability in her voice when she'd mentioned mistakes. There was so much about her he didn't understand, but he wanted to. He wanted to know everything.

When they reached the mansion, Leslie pulled to a stop at the gate, putting the car in park. He turned to her, his heart pounding as he searched for the right words.

"Here we are," he said finally.

Lina didn't move right away. Instead, she turned to face him, her eyes soft but intent. "You're a good man, Leslie."

He felt his stomach twist at her words, a mix of guilt and longing churning inside him. "I don't know about that," he said quietly.

"I do," she replied, her voice firm. She opened the door but paused, her hand lingering on the handle. "Goodnight, Leslie."

"Goodnight," he murmured, watching as she stepped out and disappeared into the night. The door closed with a soft click, but the weight of her presence remained, pressing down on him like a second skin.

Leslie sat there for a moment, staring at the closed gate. The glow of her mansion faded into the distance as he drove away, but Lina was still with him, her scent lingered in the air, her voice echoed in his mind.

7. IT'S ALL AN ACT

The heavy oak door swung open with a soft creak, and Lina stepped into the dimly lit expanse of the house. The chill of the polished marble floor seeped through her bare feet as she slipped off her heels, letting them drop carelessly by the entrance. The faint echo of her steps reverberated in the silence, a sharp contrast to the pounding bass of the nightclub she'd just left behind.

Her dress, sleek and figure-hugging, clung to her like armor, though the night had left it slightly askew. Stray tendrils of her wavy brown hair framed her face, messy from the breeze. She tried to fix it, smoothing it back with quick, impatient fingers, but it refused to cooperate. With a frustrated sigh, she abandoned the effort and placed her clutch on the granite countertop, the motion casual yet betraying the tension coiled in her body.

The living room's warm golden light bathed the space, highlighting the expensive furniture and art pieces adorning the walls.

On the leather couch, Danny Carter sat with the casual authority of a man who always owned the room. Late forties, sharp features, and eyes that missed nothing, he had the kind of presence that could either charm or intimidate—depending on which he chose to wield. His dark hair, slicked back with precision, gleamed under the light. He nursed a glass of whiskey, his shirt sleeves rolled up to reveal strong, veined forearms.

He looked up when he heard her, his face hardening instantly.

"Do you have any idea what time it is?" His voice was sharp, slicing through the air.

Lina ignored him, slipping off her jewelry as she moved toward the stairs. Her back was to him, her steps deliberate, but her shoulders stiffened at his tone.

"I didn't realize I had a curfew," she said, her voice even.

The glass in Danny's hand froze mid-sip. His eyes narrowed, and he set the drink down on the coffee table with deliberate precision before rising to his feet. His movements were slow and controlled, but there was an edge to them—a restrained anger simmering just beneath the surface.

"Don't play games with me, Lina," he said, his voice dropping into something colder. "You're out there all night, dressed like that, and you don't think I have a right to ask where you've been?"

She spun to face him, crossing her arms over her chest. Her eyes, tired but defiant, locked on his. "Dressed like what, Danny?" she said, her voice rising. "Like a prostitute? Or

41

someone who wants to feel good about herself for five minutes? God forbid I don't look miserable like you."

Danny's jaw tightened, and his knuckles whitened around the edges of his chair as if he were fighting to keep control. His voice turned to ice. "Watch your tone."

"Or what?" Lina shot back, her voice sharp and cutting. "You'll pout? Complain about how hard your life is?"

Danny's response was swift and brutal. His glass slammed onto the table, the whiskey sloshing dangerously close to the rim, and he strode toward her. His movements were no longer measured; they were predatory.

"I work my ass off to give you this life!" he growled, his voice thunderous now. "The house, the clothes, the cars—you wouldn't have any of it without me! And this is how you repay me? Parading around like a—"

"Like a what, Danny?" Lina cut him off, stepping closer, her voice daring. "Like a slut? Go ahead and say it!"

The crack of his hand across her face was deafening in the silence that followed. The force of the slap turned her head, sending a stinging heat spreading across her cheek. She stumbled, catching herself against the counter, her fingers trembling as they pressed to the reddened skin.

For a moment, the world seemed to stop. Danny froze, his chest rising and falling with uneven breaths. Guilt flickered in his eyes, but it was gone as quickly as it appeared. He turned away, his voice quiet but firm.

"Go to bed, Lina."

She didn't move. Her gaze flicked toward the corner of the room, where a small, nearly invisible surveillance camera was nestled discreetly on a shelf. It recorded everything, its silent witness adding an extra layer to the tension.

Danny pulled out his cell phone and ended the recording.

He went up to Lina and whispered, "Make sure you show this clip to Leslie."

Lina nodded, her fingers brushed her cheek again, her voice a whisper.

"Yes. Goodnight, Danny."

8. THE WEIGHT OF LONLINESS

Los Angeles was a city of noise, but inside Leslie's cramped studio apartment, the silence felt deafening. The hum of the refrigerator and the distant rumble of traffic only highlighted the emptiness of the space. He sat on the edge of his worn-out couch, his gaze drifting toward the window, where neon lights bled into the darkness like a watercolor painting left out in the rain.

Leslie knew from time to time, Uber drivers get lucky. This was the kind of encounter that only happened to others, but this time it happened to him. He shouldn't have done it. You never know about these people you pick up. They would turn around and give you a bad review, or even worse, report you to Uber for sexual harassment. Leslie knew that, but the memory of Lina's voice—soft, almost pleading—had slipped through the cracks in his resolve like water through broken stone. His desire completely over took his senses and good judgment. It wasn't just her utter beauty that drew him in, though that was undeniable. It was the way she made him feel seen, as if his existence mattered in a way it hadn't for years.

He leaned back, closing his eyes. Memories crept in, unbidden and unwelcome, pulling him under like a rip current.

Leslie had been twenty-three when his life had first derailed. Fresh out of college with a degree in communications, he'd been so sure he was on the cusp of something big. The world felt full of possibilities back then—job offers, friendships, maybe even love.

He could still remember sitting in his beat-up Honda Accord, staring at the email on his phone, the words "We regret to inform you" burning into his retinas like acid. It had been the first of many rejections.

For months, he told himself it was temporary. He'd find something. Everyone hit roadblocks. But the days turned into weeks, the weeks into months, and before he knew it, he was working part-time at a call center, fielding complaints from irate customers about cell phone service he didn't care about.

The job was supposed to be temporary. It lasted six years.

The memory shifted, and Leslie found himself standing in the kitchen of a small apartment, the air thick with the smell of burnt toast. Rachel was there, her arms crossed, her expression a mask of frustration and exhaustion. Her dark hair, which she used to wear loose and wavy, was now tied in a severe bun. She had stopped looking at him the way she used to.

"This isn't what I signed up for, Leslie," she had said, her voice tight with restrained anger. "You promised me things would get better. That you had plans. Dreams. But all you do is come home, sit on that couch, and waste away."

"I'm trying," he had replied, though even he didn't believe the words. His voice had been small, pitiful, like a man apologizing for his own existence.

"Trying isn't enough." Rachel's eyes had softened, but there was no warmth in them, only pity. "I can't keep doing this. I can't watch you drown and let you take me down with you."

She had left two weeks later. No fight. No drama. Just a note on the coffee table that said, *I'm sorry.* Leslie had found it when he came home from work, his dinner still in a brown paper bag in his hands.

He didn't cry. He hadn't cried since he was a kid. But something inside him cracked that day, a fracture that never fully healed.

By the time Leslie hit thirty, his dreams had eroded into something unrecognizable. He drove strangers around Los Angeles, his car a moving confessional booth where people unloaded their drunken regrets, their secrets, and their lies. He had become invisible, the kind of man people didn't notice unless they needed something from him. He told himself it didn't bother him, but it did. God, it did.

And then came Lina.

He opened his eyes, staring at the cracked ceiling above him. She wasn't like the others. She had seen him. Really seen him. The way she had looked at him in the rearview mirror during that first ride had been different—not with disdain or disinterest, but with a quiet intensity that had unsettled him. And when she had slid into his car for the second time, it had felt like fate. Like the universe was finally throwing him a lifeline.

But why did she choose him? The question gnawed at him, even now. What could a woman like Lina possibly see in a man like him? Maybe it didn't matter. Maybe this was his second chance, the one he'd been waiting for all along.

Or maybe it was a trap, another cruel joke from a world that seemed hell-bent on reminding him of his failures.

Leslie couldn't sleep that night. He tossed and turned on the worn couch in his apartment, his mind racing with thoughts of Lina. Her voice, her smile, her scent, her soft skin, her moist lips, the way she looked at him—it all played on a loop, refusing to fade.

Around midnight, his phone buzzed on the coffee table. He reached for it, his heart leaping when he saw her name.

Text message from Lina: "Are you awake?"

His fingers hovered over the keyboard for a moment before he typed back: "Yeah. What's up?"

Her reply came almost instantly: "I could use some company. Tomorrow morning."

Leslie stared at the screen, his pulse racing. He hesitated for only a second before responding: "Just tell me where and when."

9. THE BRUISE

The park was serene in the crisp morning air, a stark contrast to the chaos Lina had left behind. Joggers passed by with rhythmic steps, and children's laughter echoed from the nearby playground. The scent of damp grass mingled with the faint aroma of coffee drifting from a nearby vendor's cart.

Leslie sat on a bench near the edge of the path, a steaming paper cup in his hands. He wasn't really drinking it— just holding it, letting the warmth seep into his fingers as he watched the world go by. His Prius was parked nearby, but he hadn't bothered to sit in it. Somehow, the openness of the park felt less suffocating.

When Lina appeared, she was almost unrecognizable. Gone were the glamorous clothes and air of polished sophistication. She wore a pair of simple jeans, a gray hoodie that seemed a size too large, and white sneakers that had seen better days. Her hair was loosely tied back, strands escaping to frame her face. And on her left cheekbone, a faint bruise bloomed like a shadowed flower.

Leslie stood abruptly, the sight of her setting off an alarm in his chest. "Lina?"

She hesitated, then approached the bench, pulling her hoodie tighter around herself as though it might shield her from the questions she knew were coming. She sat down, folding her hands in her lap.

"What happened?" Leslie asked, his voice low but urgent.

Lina exhaled, brushing her hair back from her face. "It's... Danny."

Leslie frowned, her words not fully registering at first. "Danny?"

"My husband." She said it quietly, almost as if the words tasted bitter on her tongue.

Leslie stiffened, his mind reeling. "You're married?"

Lina nodded, her hands fidgeting with her phone. "I didn't tell you because... it's complicated."

He sank back onto the bench, running a hand through his hair. "Oh, my God. I slept with a married woman. You should have told me."

"Leslie, don't worry. He won't care."

"Does he know you're here?"

"No," she said quickly. "He's at work. He doesn't know anything."

Her tone was meant to be reassuring, but it didn't soothe the storm in Leslie's chest. The bruise on her face, the way she held herself—it all pointed to a story she wasn't fully telling him. And that story had something to do with Danny.

Lina stared at her hands, the knuckles pale as her fingers fidgeted with the edge of her phone case. The park around them felt distant, the laughter of children and the rhythmic pounding of joggers' feet blending into white noise. Leslie leaned forward, elbows resting on his knees, his coffee forgotten on the ground between his feet.

He couldn't take his eyes off the faint bruise shadowing her cheek. It was an ugly contrast to her otherwise delicate features, a silent testament to violence he couldn't comprehend.

"What did he do to you?" he asked softly, his voice a mix of concern and barely suppressed anger.

Lina hesitated, her throat working as she tried to find the words. "It's not always like this," she said finally, her voice trembling. "He's not always..."

"Not always what?" Leslie pressed, his tone sharper than he intended.

Her head snapped up, her gaze meeting his. There was something raw in her expression—a mixture of shame, anger, and exhaustion.

"He's not always a monster, okay? Sometimes, he's the man I married. Sometimes, he's kind. But then there are days when..." She trailed off, swallowing hard.

Leslie shook his head, his fists clenching on his knees. "Lina, this isn't okay. None of it is. You shouldn't have to live like this."

Lina's lips pressed into a tight line, and she looked away. "You think I don't know that?"

"Then why stay?" Leslie asked, his voice rising slightly. "You're smart. You're strong. Why let him do this to you? I'm assuming this isn't the first time."

Her shoulders stiffened, and she turned back to him, her eyes blazing. "Do you have any idea what it's like to be trapped?" she snapped. "He controls everything, Leslie. The money, the house, my entire life. If I leave, I have nothing. Nowhere to go."

Leslie flinched at the venom in her tone but forced himself to stay calm. "There has to be a way out," he said, his voice quieter now. "You don't have to do this alone."

Lina let out a bitter laugh, her fingers tightening around her phone. "You think it's that easy? To just walk away? Danny isn't the kind of man who lets go. He'd find me, and when he did..." She shuddered, her words trailing off.

The thought of what Danny might do made Leslie's stomach twist. He leaned closer, his voice low and steady. "Then we make sure he doesn't get the chance."

Lina froze, her eyes narrowing. "What are you saying?"

Leslie hesitated, realizing the weight of his own words. "I'm saying we figure something out. Together."

A long silence stretched between them, the tension palpable. Lina's gaze dropped to her lap, her expression unreadable. Finally, she spoke, her voice barely above a whisper. "I've been recording him."

Leslie blinked, caught off guard. "Recording him? How?"

"Every time he does something like this," she said, gesturing vaguely to her cheek, "I make sure I have evidence. Videos. Audio. Something to prove what he's really like."

She unlocked her phone and scrolled through her files before handing it to Leslie. On the screen was a video thumbnail, the timestamp recent. He hesitated before tapping it.

The grainy footage showed Danny pacing the living room, his voice sharp and accusatory. "You're late again! You think I don't notice?" His movements were jerky, erratic. Then, without warning, his hand lashed out, the slap echoing through the speakers. Lina stumbled back, clutching her face, her expression stunned.

The video ended abruptly.

Leslie stared at the screen, his jaw tight. "That bastard," he muttered.

Lina reached out, taking the phone from him. Her fingers trembled slightly as she locked the screen and slipped it back into her pocket. "It's not enough," she said. "Even with this, he could spin it. Make me look like the problem."

"You don't know that," Leslie argued. "You could take this to the police—"

"And then what?" Lina interrupted, her voice breaking. "Danny's reputation would be ruined. He'd lose everything. And then he'd come for me. Do you think he'd let me get away with destroying his life?"

Leslie ran a hand through his hair, frustration simmering just beneath the surface. "So you're just going to stay? Let him keep doing this to you?"

"No," Lina said, her voice firmer now. "I'm not going to stay."

Her words hung in the air, heavy with implication. Leslie turned to her, searching her face for answers. "What are you saying?"

Lina looked away, her hands clasped tightly in her lap. "Sometimes," she said slowly, "I think the only way out is if... if he wasn't here anymore."

The words sent a chill down Leslie's spine. "You're not serious," he said, his voice low.

Lina didn't respond. She just hugged herself, her body curling inward as though to shield herself from the weight of what she'd just said.

"Lina," Leslie said, his tone gentle but firm. "Killing him... that's not the answer."

She turned to him, her eyes shining with unshed tears. "I don't want to kill him, Leslie," she whispered. "But I don't know what else to do."

For a moment, neither of them spoke. Leslie's mind raced, the enormity of the situation crashing over him. He reached out, placing a hand on her shoulder. "We'll figure something out," he said quietly. "I promise."

Lina stared at him, her lip trembling. Slowly, she nodded. "Thank you," she whispered.

As they sat there on the bench, Leslie's arm was around her, the world continued to move around them. But for Leslie, everything had shifted. He didn't know what he was getting himself into, but one thing was clear—he couldn't walk away from Lina now. Not when she needed him most.

10. NUMBERS DON'T LIE

The fluorescent lights buzzed softly in the background as James Reid sat at his polished desk, the surface almost sterile in its organization. The sleek, modern office was a testament to success—glass walls overlooking the bustling floor of Cater, Reid, Greene Accounting Firm. But at this moment, success felt far away. James rubbed his temples, staring at the spreadsheet on his laptop screen. The rows of numbers mocked him, their stark reality undeniable.

Six million dollars. Missing.

"How is this even possible?" he muttered, his voice low but tight with frustration.

Rebecca Greene, standing just behind him, leaned over to examine the screen. She furrowed her brow, her lips pressed into a thin line. She wasn't prone to overreaction—calm, calculated responses were her forte. But this? This was troubling.

"That's... six million dollars?" she said finally, her voice tinged with disbelief.

James exhaled sharply, swiveling his chair to face her. "Nowhere to be found. And before you ask, no—the audit logs don't show anything."

Rebecca straightened, crossing her arms. Her dark brown eyes flicked back to the screen, as if willing the numbers to change. They didn't.

"It has to be a mistake," she said, though the words lacked conviction. "Some kind of system error."

James's expression hardened, his distinguished features etched with skepticism. "You really think a 'system error' made six million dollars disappear?"

Rebecca bit her lip, a nervous habit she thought she'd broken years ago. "Okay," she admitted. "Let's say it's not an error. Who's handling these accounts?"

James turned his chair slightly, his gaze drifting through the glass walls of his office. His eyes landed on Danny Carter, seated at his desk a few yards away. Danny looked as composed as ever, his dark hair slicked back with the precision of a man who didn't leave anything to chance. His fingers moved quickly across the keyboard, his posture relaxed, exuding an air of effortless confidence.

James sighed and rubbed his temples again. "Rebecca," he said quietly, "look into it."

The conference room was sleek and sterile, its glass walls offering a clear view of the bustling office beyond. The

Cater, Reid, Greene logo etched onto the door gleamed in the morning sunlight.

Inside, the atmosphere was decidedly less bright.

Danny sat at the head of the table, his cup of coffee steaming gently in front of him. He leaned back slightly, his dark suit impeccably tailored, his polished shoes glinting faintly under the overhead lights. Across from him, James and Rebecca sat side by side, their laptops open, notepads ready. There was a palpable tension in the air, like the faint hum before a storm.

Danny sipped his coffee, his sharp eyes flicking between them. He didn't miss much. Something was off.

"So," he began, setting the cup down with a deliberate clink, "what's this meeting about?"

James cleared his throat, adjusting his glasses. He glanced briefly at Rebecca, as if silently asking for backup, before speaking.

"Just an internal review," he said, his tone attempting casualness. "Standard procedure, you know."

Danny raised an eyebrow, leaning back in his chair. His expression remained calm, but his gaze was penetrating. "I didn't realize we were auditing ourselves now."

Rebecca offered a polite chuckle, though her voice remained measured. "Not an audit, exactly. Just a deeper look into client accounts—high-level stuff."

Danny folded his hands in front of him, his gaze locking on James. "And my accounts are part of this 'deeper look'?"

James hesitated, then nodded. "You're handling some of the firm's biggest clients, Danny. It's routine to make sure everything's in order, especially with the recent... discrepancies."

Danny's jaw tightened imperceptibly. "Discrepancies?"

Rebecca jumped in quickly, her voice calm but pointed. "There's nothing concrete, Danny. Just a few numbers that didn't quite add up in the quarterly reports. Could be anything— a software glitch, a clerical error. We just want to be thorough."

Danny studied them for a moment, his expression unreadable. But there was a shift in his demeanor—a subtle hardening of his posture, the faintest narrowing of his eyes.

"And you decided to start with my accounts?" he asked, his tone deceptively smooth.

James leaned forward slightly, his hands clasped on the table. "Danny, no one's pointing fingers here. We're just covering all our bases."

"It's nothing personal," Rebecca added, her tone meant to soothe.

Danny forced a smile, though it didn't reach his eyes. "Of course," he said, his voice like silk stretched over steel. "Nothing personal."

He stood abruptly, straightening his tie with practiced precision. The movement was fluid, deliberate, as though reminding them of his authority. "Let me know if you find anything," he said, "we're gonna upgrade our system, right?" His voice laced with thinly veiled condescension.

As he walked to the door, he paused, one hand resting on the handle. Without turning back, he added, "But I'd be careful about making baseless assumptions. It can be... damaging."

The unspoken threat hung in the air long after the door clicked shut behind him.

James exhaled, running a hand through his silver hair. Rebecca crossed her arms, her brow furrowed.

"He knows something," she said quietly.

James nodded grimly. "The question is—how much?"

11. THE INVESTIGATOR

The office buzzed with life, a cacophony of ringing phones, clicking keyboards, and murmured conversations that blended into an ambient hum. Rows of cubicles lined the floor, each one housing agents hunched over their computers, lost in a world of claims, policies, and payouts. Norman Fields sat at his desk, his sharp eyes glued to the grainy surveillance footage playing on his screen.

The video showed a man hoisting a heavy box onto the back of a truck. Sweat glistened on the man's forehead, but his movements were fluid and strong, the kind that came from years of physical labor. Norman clicked to rewind the footage, slowing it down to watch the same scene again. He leaned forward, his jaw tightening.

"Disability claim, huh?" Norman muttered to himself, jotting notes in a well-worn leather notebook. "Impressive form for a bad back."

He clicked again, pulling up the claimant's file. A headshot of the man appeared alongside a detailed breakdown of his permanent disability claim. Norman's lips curled into a faint smirk as he reached for his phone.

"It's Norman," he said, his voice low and calm. "Got a case of blatant fraud. You'll want to see this—our claimant's moonlighting as a mover. I'll send over the footage. We should move to deny the claim and flag him for further review."

On the other end, someone murmured their agreement before the call ended. Norman leaned back in his chair, closing the file with a satisfying snap. He allowed himself a moment of quiet triumph, his gaze drifting to the framed photo on his desk.

It showed a younger Norman, standing proudly with an award committee, shaking hands as a plaque in the foreground read: "Excellence in Insurance Investigation."

Norman exhaled and straightened his tie, stepping out of his cubicle. As he walked through the bustling office, passing rows of agents buried in their work, Karen, the front desk assistant, flagged him down with a raised hand.

"Norman, got something for you," she said, holding up a thin file.

He approached, his curiosity piqued as she handed it over.

"Stevens wants you to personally review this one," Karen explained. "High-value payout, double indemnity clause. Said you might know the guy."

Norman flipped open the file, his sharp gaze scanning the bold name at the top: Daniel Carter. His lips twitched into a slight, knowing smirk.

"Carter," he murmured. "It's been a while."

Karen raised an eyebrow. "You know him?"

Norman nodded absently, already flipping through the policy details. "I sold him this policy years ago. Double indemnity... smart guy. A little too careful, if you ask me."

Karen didn't press further, though her expression betrayed curiosity. "Stevens said to prioritize it. Big money on the line."

"Got it," Norman said, closing the file. His mind was already turning over the implications as he walked back to his desk.

12. COFFEE AND COVER STORIES

The neighborhood coffee shop bustled with quiet energy. The hiss of steaming milk and the soft clatter of ceramic cups filled the air, blending with the low hum of conversation. Outside, the late afternoon sun cast long shadows over the sidewalk tables, where Norman sat, sipping a black coffee. His tailored suit was sharp but understated, his demeanor professional yet approachable. Beside him, a polished leather briefcase rested against the chair leg.

He checked his watch, then glanced toward the street. Right on time, Danny appeared, cutting a confident figure in a tailored navy suit. His stride was purposeful, but as he approached the table, a flicker of unease crossed his otherwise composed face.

"Norman Fields," Danny said, extending a hand. "Long time, no see."

Norman stood, shaking his hand firmly. "Danny Carter. Still running the show, I see. Thanks for meeting on short notice."

Danny offered a polite smile as he sat, setting his phone on the table within easy reach. "You made it sound important. Everything good on your end?"

Norman chuckled, pulling a folder from his briefcase and setting it between them. "Oh, nothing serious. Just a routine review. High-value policies like yours get flagged for a check-in every now and then. Company protocol."

Danny's smile remained polite, but Norman didn't miss the slight tightening of his jaw. "I see. Double indemnity policies tend to draw attention, huh?"

"You'd be surprised," Norman said, leaning back. "Big payouts make everyone nervous—claimants, the company, and sometimes even the policyholders."

Danny chuckled, but the sound was hollow. "Well, I hope everything's in order. I haven't exactly had to use it... yet."

Norman laughed, flipping open the file. "Everything looks fine. Just a few updates to confirm. Same beneficiary as before—your wife, Lina?"

"Last time I checked," Danny replied smoothly.

Norman jotted something down, his pen gliding over the page with deliberate ease. "Business keeping you busy?"

"Always," Danny said, relaxing slightly. "My partners and I have been swamped, but that's how you know things are going well, right?"

Norman raised an eyebrow, sipping his coffee. "Good to hear. You always struck me as the type to keep all the plates spinning. Though, I imagine that comes with its fair share of headaches."

Danny leaned forward slightly, his voice measured. "It's all about balance, Norman. You'd be surprised what you can manage when you keep a clear head."

Norman smiled, setting down his cup. "Well, like I said, nothing serious. Just doing my rounds. Let me know if there are any changes or concerns—new assets, big purchases, big plans, anything that might affect the policy."

"You'll be the first to know," Danny said, his tone light but firm.

Norman rose, extending a hand. Danny stood as well, shaking it firmly, though the faintest hint of unease lingered in his expression.

"Good seeing you, Danny. Take care," Norman said with a faint smile.

As Norman walked away, Danny sat back down, staring at the untouched coffee in front of him. The polished veneer of confidence he always wore cracked slightly as his thoughts raced, his hand instinctively moving to check his phone.

13. A QUESTION OF DESIRE

The GPS voice droned monotonously in the background of Leslie's Prius as he navigated the tangled streets of Los Angeles. His face was set in a distracted frown, the weight of unspoken thoughts pressing heavily on his mind. The city's endless motion surrounded him—cars whizzing by, pedestrians weaving through traffic—but Leslie felt detached, as if he were moving in slow motion while the world rushed on without him.

A ping from the app brought him back to the present. Moments later, the back doors of his car opened, and a young couple climbed in, their laughter spilling into the confined space. They barely noticed him, their focus entirely on each other.

"Did you see how beautiful that place was?" the woman gushed, her eyes shining. "We should go back next weekend."

"Definitely," her partner replied, squeezing her hand. Their shared joy filled the car, an unspoken intimacy that seemed to wrap around them like a cocoon.

Leslie glanced at them in the rearview mirror, his gaze softening for a moment. But as he watched their happiness, a faint pang of envy flickered in his chest. He turned his eyes back to the road, his jaw tightening. Happiness like that wasn't meant for people like him.

14. A FRAGILE INVITATION

The coffee in Leslie's hands had gone cold by the time Lina's name lit up his phone screen. He picked it up without hesitation, his heart skipping as he answered. "Lina?"

Her voice on the other end was soft but carried an undercurrent of urgency. "Can we meet? There's something I need to tell you."

The bar was dimly lit, the quiet hum of soft jazz mingling with the faint clink of glasses. Leslie sat at a small corner table, fidgeting with the edges of a napkin. His nerves were frayed, his thoughts tangled with questions and possibilities. When Lina entered, his breath hitched.

Even in simplicity—a black dress that clung to her form without ostentation, her hair loosely framing her face—she commanded attention. She moved with purpose, but there was something else in her expression, a vulnerability that made her seem more human, more reachable.

"Hope I didn't keep you waiting," she said as she slipped into the seat across from him, signaling the bartender with a quick wave.

Leslie shook his head, his mouth dry. "No, not at all."

Lina folded her hands on the table, leaning slightly forward. "I couldn't stop thinking about our last conversation."

Leslie's resolve crumbled under the weight of her gaze. "You... shouldn't have to live like this," he said, his voice thick with sincerity.

Her hand moved across the table, resting lightly on his. "I won't. Not if you're with me."

The words hit him like a punch, scattering his thoughts. He stared at her, his emotions battling between doubt and longing. "Lina, I'm just... a regular guy. I can't give you the life you deserve. I don't have—"

She leaned in, cutting him off with a whisper. "I don't care about all that. I chose you because I know you'll treat me well." Her voice dropped lower, her tone both pleading and seductive. "We could have a life together, Leslie. Just you and me."

Her words wrapped around him, melting his defenses. When she leaned closer, brushing her lips against his, he hesitated for only a moment before giving in. The kiss deepened, her hands sliding to the back of his neck as his thoughts dissolved in the heat of the moment.

The neon sign outside the roadside motel flickered faintly, casting an eerie glow over the parking lot. "Vacancy," it proclaimed, the buzzing hum of its light filling the silence. Leslie pulled into a spot under a dim streetlamp, his Prius coming to a

69

stop with a slight jolt. The place was quiet, the kind of isolation that promised secrets would be kept.

Inside the car, Leslie gripped the steering wheel so tightly his knuckles turned white. His breathing was shallow, his thoughts a whirlwind of doubt and desire. Beside him, Lina sat quietly, her presence magnetic. Her gaze drifted to the motel, then back to him.

"Let's go inside," she said softly.

Leslie shook his head, his voice cracking. "Lina, we shouldn't..."

"Why not?" she asked, her voice steady, though her eyes glimmered with vulnerability. She reached out, her hand resting lightly on his arm.

"Because you're married!" The words burst out of him, sharp and accusing, lingering in the air like a storm cloud.

Lina flinched at the tone, then looked down, her voice trembling. "Married?" She laughed bitterly. "Leslie, Danny doesn't care about me. He buries himself in work and barely notices when I'm home. He's probably going to hurt me again when I walk through the door."

Leslie turned to her, his eyes dark with anger. "You can't let him do that to you! I can't imagine how he could abuse you like that."

She exhaled shakily, brushing a strand of hair from her face. "Yes, he's angry and cruel. But as a husband? That ended a long time ago. We're practically separated. There's no love left. No connection."

Leslie's grip on the wheel loosened, his resolve wavering. "But what if he finds out?"

Lina shook her head, her voice firm. "He won't. And even if he did, what's he going to do? He's too busy with his precious career to care about what I do."

She reached out, placing her hand over his, gently pulling it away from the wheel. Her touch was warm, her voice soft. "Leslie. I need you. I want you."

The motel room was modest but clean, its beige walls illuminated by the warm glow of a bedside lamp. Lina closed the door behind her, the click of the lock sounding louder than it should have. She turned to face Leslie, her expression a mixture of longing and determination.

"You're the only one who's ever made me feel seen," she said, her voice barely above a whisper.

Leslie stood frozen near the door, his nerves fraying at the edges. "Lina, this still feels... wrong."

She stepped closer, her hands finding their way to his chest. "It's not wrong when it feels this right."

Her eyes shimmered, brimming with what seemed like emotion. Leslie wanted to believe it, needed to believe it. "I haven't felt this way in years," she continued. "With you, I feel alive. Wanted."

Her words dissolved the last of his defenses. When she leaned up to kiss him, he didn't pull away. Instead, he wrapped his arms around her, letting himself get lost in her.

As the kiss deepened, she began slipping out of her dress, the fabric pooling at her feet. Her body, lit by the warm glow of the lamp, drew him in completely.

His reservations, his doubts—all of it crumbled as desire took over. They moved to the bed together, the shadows on the walls blending into one another as they succumbed to the moment.

15. A BRAND NEW LIFE

The upscale clothing store gleamed with luxury, its polished floors reflecting the soft golden light from overhead fixtures. Rows of designer suits, crisp shirts, and sleek casual wear filled the space, each piece seeming to exude sophistication. Leslie stood near the entrance, his worn jeans and basic T-shirt a stark contrast to the store's refined atmosphere. His unease was palpable as he watched Lina glide confidently through the racks, her fingers brushing over fabric with practiced ease.

"We can't have you looking like this forever, Leslie," Lina said, her tone playful but tinged with something more serious.

Leslie glanced down at himself, frowning slightly. "What's wrong with the way I look?"

Lina turned to him, her lips curving into a soft smile. "Nothing... if you plan to keep driving strangers around for tips."

The words stung, but before Leslie could respond, she stepped closer, holding up a tailored blazer. "But that's not who you are anymore," she continued, smoothing the fabric with her hands. "You're with me now. I want to dress you up. Like a lover boy."

Her touch lingered as she handed him the blazer, her gaze locking with his. Leslie hesitated, then took it, his fingers brushing against hers. "Try this on," she said, her voice coaxing.

The fitting room was small but elegant, its full-length mirror reflecting an image Leslie barely recognized. The blazer fit him perfectly, the dark fabric accentuating his broad shoulders and lean frame. For a moment, he stood straighter, his usual slouch replaced by an unfamiliar confidence.

"Let me see!" Lina called from outside.

Leslie stepped out, and Lina's face lit up with approval. She approached him, smoothing the fabric on his shoulder with a meticulous hand. "Now that's more like it," she said, her eyes glimmering with satisfaction.

Leslie glanced at a nearby mirror, seeing himself transformed. For the first time, he looked like someone who belonged in places like this, someone who could hold his own in a world far removed from his old life. He smiled faintly, unsure if he liked what he saw—or if he was simply mesmerized by Lina's vision of him.

The dealership lot sparkled under the midday sun, rows of gleaming cars polished to perfection. Lina led Leslie across the asphalt with the same air of confidence she'd shown in the clothing store, her heels clicking against the pavement. They stopped in front of a candy-apple red convertible Mustang, its curves sleek and seductive.

Leslie's jaw dropped. "You're joking, right?"

Lina grinned, holding up a set of keys. "Not at all. Every new man deserves a new ride."

He stared at the car, his hand trembling slightly as he ran his fingers along the smooth, cool surface. The reflection of the sun off the paint made it seem almost alive. "This... this is too much, Lina."

She stepped closer, her voice dropping to a sultry whisper.

"Nothing's too much for my man." She leaned in, her breath warm against his cheek. "Besides," she added with a wicked smile, "this thing makes me wet."

The heat in her words made Leslie's face flush. He finally allowed himself to smile, catching the keys as she tossed them his way.

The apartment was like something out of a dream. Floor-to-ceiling windows framed the glittering Los Angeles skyline, casting the modern, spacious interior in a warm, golden glow. Boxes of new items Lina had insisted on buying were scattered around the pristine space, each one a symbol of the life she was building for him—or molding him into.

Leslie stood in the center of the living room, his hands resting on his hips as he took it all in. "I... I don't know what to say," he murmured.

Lina stepped behind him, her hands sliding down his arms. "You could start with, 'Thank you, Lina. You're amazing.'"

Leslie chuckled, turning to face her. "Thank you, Lina. You're amazing."

Her smile deepened, but her eyes held a trace of something deeper—something calculating. "You deserve this, Leslie," she said, her voice soft and intimate. "You deserve more than that old life you were living."

Her hands rested on his chest, her touch firm but gentle. "And we deserve to be happy together."

The weight of her words pressed down on him. Leslie opened his mouth to respond, but before he could, Lina leaned up and kissed him softly. The warmth of her lips erased his hesitation, pulling him into her orbit once again.

"Lina..." he began, but she silenced him with another kiss, her arms wrapping around his neck. She guided him toward the couch, her intentions clear.

"Let's christen this place," she whispered, her voice laced with both desire and command.

Leslie let go of his reservations, his hands sliding to her waist as she pulled him down onto the plush cushions. Their movements were slow and deliberate, the passion between them building as the light from the windows bathed the room in a golden haze. Lina's clothes fell away, her body revealed in the soft glow of the evening light. Leslie's kisses trailed across her skin, her breath hitching with each touch.

The dining table was set for two, candles flickering softly in the center. Plates with the remnants of a home-cooked meal sat between Leslie and Lina as they leaned back in their chairs, glasses of red wine in hand. The apartment felt warm and intimate, the city lights twinkling beyond the windows like distant stars.

Leslie swirled the wine in his glass, glancing at Lina with a smile. "Okay, I have to say it—this was amazing. I didn't know you could cook like this."

Lina chuckled, her eyes sparkling as she sipped her wine. "There's a lot you don't know about me, Leslie."

"Well," he said, raising his glass in a mock toast, "if this is one of your secrets, keep them coming."

She smiled, leaning forward slightly. "You're easy to cook for. You actually appreciate the effort."

Leslie's gaze drifted around the apartment, his smile faltering slightly. "I still can't believe this is my life now."

Lina rested her chin on her hand, her voice soft but firm. "Get used to it."

The words hung in the air, filled with a promise that Leslie wasn't sure he fully understood.

He looked back at her, his hesitation melting under the intensity of her gaze. "You make it hard not to," he admitted.

Lina stood, setting her glass down as she moved behind him. Her hands rested on his shoulders, her touch firm but comforting. "You've earned this, Leslie. A fresh start. A new life." She leaned closer, her breath warm against his ear. "With me."

Leslie tilted his head back to look at her, his face softening. "You really believe we can have that?"

She smiled, sliding her hands down his arms and coaxing him to stand. "I don't just believe it," she said, her voice low and sure. "I know it."

Her lips brushed against his as she led him toward the couch, the city lights casting long shadows across the room. They kissed slowly, deliberately, the moment heavy with both passion and the weight of unspoken promises.

"This is just the beginning," Lina whispered, her words sinking into Leslie like a vow.

The city sparkled outside, a stark contrast to the shadows growing within.

16. BREAKING POINTS

The opulent living room of Danny and Lina's mansion was bathed in subdued light, the chandeliers casting long, flickering shadows on the high ceilings. The polished marble floors gleamed, reflecting the soft glow of the room's understated elegance.

On the couch, Lina sat flipping through a magazine, her movements slow and deliberate, her expression calm but carefully rehearsed. Beneath her poised demeanor, a knot of tension coiled tightly in her chest.

The quiet was broken by the low rumble of a car pulling into the driveway. Lina didn't flinch, but her fingers froze on the glossy pages. Moments later, the front door swung open with a force that made the hinges groan. Danny stepped inside, his briefcase in one hand, his tie loosened. His sharp eyes swept the room, landing on the shopping bags scattered near the staircase. His expression darkened.

"More shopping, Lina?" he asked, his voice low but laced with accusation.

Lina glanced up, her tone light but carrying an edge of defiance. "Just a few things."

Danny's jaw tightened as he dropped his briefcase onto the side table with a loud thud. The sound reverberated through the room, making her flinch despite herself. His voice rose, sharp and cutting.

"A few things? Do you think I'm blind? Fifty-two thousand dollars for a convertible Mustang? Twelve thousand dollars for an apartment deposit? Another ten thousand for clothes and bags?" He gestured toward the staircase, his movements abrupt and angry.

Lina closed the magazine with deliberate slowness, her calm façade beginning to crack. "It's my money too, Danny," she said evenly. "Or have you forgotten?"

Danny stepped closer, his face twisting into a sneer. "Your money?" He let out a bitter laugh. "You've been burning through cash like we're made of it. I don't even see the car! What the hell are you up to, Lina?"

Lina rose from the couch with measured grace, her chin tilted up as her eyes locked with his. Her fury was quiet but palpable.

"What I'm up to?" she repeated, her voice trembling slightly. "Maybe I'm just tired, Danny. Tired of being ignored. Tired of being treated like furniture while you play accountant to the world."

He closed the remaining distance between them, the tension crackling in the air. "Don't push me, Lina," he warned, his voice dropping to a dangerous growl.

When he grabbed her wrist, his grip wasn't painful, but it was forceful enough to make her gasp. She yanked her arm back, her movement exaggerated as though the contact had hurt more than it truly had. "Let go of me, Danny!" she cried, her voice loud enough to carry through the cavernous room.

Danny released her wrist with a sharp motion, his face hardening. "I'm warning you," he said, his tone ice-cold. "Enough with the games."

Without waiting for a response, he turned and stormed upstairs, his heavy footsteps echoing on the marble staircase. Lina stood frozen for a moment, her chest rising and falling as she fought to control her breathing. When she finally moved, it was with calculated precision. She rubbed her wrist, applying just enough pressure to redden the skin. Her lips pressed into a thin line as she glanced toward the corner of the room, where a small, concealed camera recorded everything.

The master bedroom was as lavish as the rest of the mansion, its floor-to-ceiling windows offering a breathtaking view of the city lights. Lina entered with purpose, heading straight to the walk-in closet. She yanked a suitcase from the shelf, throwing it onto the bed. Her hands moved quickly, pulling clothes from hangers and shoving them into the open case. Each movement was sharp and deliberate, her lips pressed into a tight line of fury.

Danny appeared in the doorway, leaning against the frame with his arms crossed. His expression was a mix of disdain and amusement, his presence filling the room with menace.

"You think you can just walk out of here?" he asked, his voice dripping with condescension. "That you'll survive without me?"

Lina ignored him, her movements unrelenting as she zipped the suitcase shut.

Danny pushed off the doorframe, taking a step closer. "Let me guess," he said, his tone turning venomous. "You're going to see that bastard, aren't you?"

For a fraction of a second, Lina froze, her hands gripping the suitcase handle. She didn't answer, but her silence spoke volumes.

Danny's voice rose, the anger in it unchecked now. "Go ahead, Lina. Walk out that door tonight, and don't you ever come back!"

Her grip on the suitcase tightened as she turned to face him, her eyes blazing with defiance. "As you wish," she said, her voice trembling but resolute.

As she moved toward the door, Danny grabbed her arm. This time, his hand lashed out, striking her across the face. The sound of the slap echoed in the room like a gunshot. Lina staggered, her free hand flying to her cheek as her eyes filled with tears—not from the pain, but from the calculated fury it took to remain composed.

She met his gaze, her head held high, and without another word, she walked past him. Her footsteps echoed down the staircase, each one a defiant challenge. Danny didn't follow, but his voice rang out from the bedroom like a curse.

82

"You're going to regret this, Lina!" he bellowed. "You hear me? You're going to regret it!"

17. THE PERFECT WITNESS

The knock at Leslie's apartment door startled him from his thoughts. He crossed the room quickly, opening the door to find Lina standing there. She held a suitcase in one hand, her face flushed with emotion. A faint redness on her cheek hinted at the confrontation she'd just left behind.

"Lina?" Leslie said, his voice filled with concern. "What happened?"

She stepped inside, setting the suitcase down with trembling hands. Her voice was shaky, a mix of anger and desperation. "I couldn't stay there anymore, Leslie. He... he's gone too far this time."

Leslie stared at her, his protective instincts flaring. "What did he do?"

Lina pulled out her phone, her fingers moving quickly as she brought up the video. She held it out to Leslie, her hand trembling. "You have to see this."

Leslie took the phone, his jaw tightening as he watched the footage. Danny's angry voice filled the room, followed by the sight of him grabbing her wrist and the slap that came soon after. Leslie's fists clenched at his sides.

"That bastard," he muttered, his voice low and dangerous. "Lina, you absolutely have to get out of this toxic situation!"

She wiped a tear from her cheek, looking up at him with pleading eyes. "Leslie, I need you. I can't do this alone."

Leslie's jaw tightened, his mind racing. He placed a reassuring hand on her shoulder. "You're safe now. We'll do something about it."

Lina leaned into him, her vulnerability drawing him deeper into her orbit. As Leslie held her, his thoughts swirled with anger, guilt, and a growing determination to protect her at any cost.

18. THE PRESSURE'S ON

James's office overlooked the city skyline, the sprawling view a stark contrast to the storm brewing inside. The sleek, functional space, typically a sanctuary of order and precision, felt claustrophobic as James flipped through a stack of printed financial statements. Each line of text seemed to mock him, a riddle he couldn't solve. He rubbed his temples, the weight of the discovery pressing down on him.

Rebecca stood behind him, leaning over his shoulder as she pointed to a highlighted column on the spreadsheet. Her brow furrowed, and her usually calm demeanor cracked with unease.

"There it is again," she said, her voice tight. "Another unaccounted transfer."

James exhaled sharply, tossing the papers onto the desk. "That makes five transactions in the last eleven months. All routed through the same shell company."

Rebecca took a seat across from him, opening her laptop and pulling up the digital records. "We're talking millions, James. Are we sure this isn't just some kind of bookkeeping error?"

He shook his head, his gaze hard. "Not at this level. These transactions were deliberate."

Rebecca leaned back, her arms crossing as she absorbed the gravity of his words. "And the fact that Danny's name is tied to the authorizations?" she asked carefully.

James hesitated, his expression conflicted. "It doesn't help," he admitted. "Danny's been... distracted lately. Showing up late, leaving early. He's not the same guy we started this firm with."

Rebecca frowned, her worry deepening. "You don't think he's actually behind this, do you?"

"I don't know," James said, his voice low. "But something's not right."

Rebecca's fingers drummed on the edge of her laptop. "If we confront him and we're wrong, it could blow up in our faces. This kind of accusation..."

James leaned forward, resting his elbows on the desk. "We're not confronting him. Not yet."

He opened a drawer and pulled out a simple business card, sliding it across the desk to Rebecca. The name Michael Langston, CPA was printed in bold.

"There's a forensic accountant I worked with years ago," James explained. "He's discreet. Thorough. Let's have him take a closer look before we make any moves."

Rebecca picked up the card, turning it over in her fingers. "Do you really think we need to bring someone in?"

James's expression was grim. "If I'm right, we're talking about more than just missing money. This kind of amount could bring down the whole firm."

Rebecca nodded slowly, the weight of the situation sinking in. "I'll call him."

The restaurant was elegant, its atmosphere buzzing with soft conversations and the delicate clink of silverware. A string quartet played faintly in the background, their melody blending seamlessly into the refined ambiance.

At a corner table, Danny Carter sat with James and Rebecca, a glass of red wine in his hand. His tailored suit was impeccable, but his preoccupied gaze betrayed his distraction.

"It's been a while since the three of us did this," Rebecca said, her voice light as she smiled at Danny. "We're always so buried in work."

James raised his glass. "To our success—and to taking a damn moment to breathe."

Danny forced a smile, clinking glasses with them. "To that," he said, his tone cordial but distant.

As they sipped their wine, Rebecca set her glass down and leaned in slightly. "How are things at home, Danny?" she asked, her tone casual but probing. "You've seemed... distracted lately."

Danny's smile tightened, and he shifted in his seat, swirling his wine absently. "You know how it is—work never really leaves you alone."

James exchanged a subtle glance with Rebecca but kept his voice light. "You've been leaving work early these days. Must be nice to have a bit more balance."

Danny's eyes flicked to him, narrowing slightly. "Just trying to keep the wife happy," he replied, his tone edged with something harder. "She's... demanding, to say the least."

Rebecca laughed lightly, though her gaze lingered on Danny's face, studying him. "Well, if you ever need to talk, you know where to find us."

Danny nodded, his expression guarded. "Thanks, Rebecca. I appreciate it."

The conversation shifted to lighter topics—industry gossip, client anecdotes—but the tension remained. Danny's gaze flicked between his partners, suspicion flickering behind his otherwise composed demeanor. He swirled his wine again, his mind clearly elsewhere.

19. SUSPICION THICKENS

James's office felt more oppressive than usual as Michael Langston sat across from him and Rebecca, the air heavy with anticipation. Michael, hired by James, a no-nonsense forensic accountant in his late 40s, sifted through stacks of financial records spread across the desk. His brow furrowed in concentration as his pen tapped rhythmically against the papers.

"There are definitely irregularities here," Michael said finally, his voice calm but tinged with gravity. "Transfers to offshore accounts, suspicious vendor payments... But whoever did this knew how to cover their tracks."

Rebecca leaned forward, her fingers gripping the edge of the desk. "Is there anything that ties it to Danny?" she asked, her voice tight.

Michael hesitated, setting his pen down. "Nothing concrete," he admitted. "The transactions were routed through multiple layers of accounts. It's... clever. Almost too clever for someone working alone."

James frowned, processing the implication. "You're saying it could be someone else?"

Michael shrugged slightly. "It's possible. But without direct evidence, all we have is circumstantial. Whoever did this knows the system well enough to exploit its weaknesses. It's not amateur work."

Rebecca exchanged a glance with James, worry etched across her face. "So what do we do?" she asked.

Michael leaned back in his chair, crossing his arms. "Keep an eye on him. If Danny's involved, he'll slip up eventually. But for now, you need to proceed cautiously. If you act without proof, it could backfire."

James nodded slowly, his jaw tightening. "Thank you, Michael."

"In the meantime, I have a tool that may be able to find the truth a lot faster. Let me set it up next week." Michael said with certainty.

As Michael gathered his materials, Rebecca stared at the pile of records, her mind racing. The stakes were higher than ever, and the truth felt just out of reach.

20. THE IRREFUSABLE OFFER

The rooftop bar was perched atop one of Santa Monica's boutique hotels, its open-air terrace offering sweeping views of the Pacific Ocean. Twinkling string lights hung overhead, casting a soft glow over the sleek, modern seating arrangements. A cool breeze carried the faint scent of saltwater, mingling with the muted hum of conversation and the occasional clink of glasses.

Norman adjusted his tie as he stepped out of the elevator, his eyes scanning the crowd. It wasn't the kind of place he frequented—too trendy, too polished—but Danny had insisted. And Norman, as much as he hated to admit it, was curious.

He spotted Danny at a corner table, positioned just far enough from the other patrons to ensure privacy. Danny was nursing a glass of bourbon, his tailored suit immaculate, his posture relaxed.

"Norman," Danny greeted with a smile as the older man approached. "Glad you could make it. Can I get you a drink?"

Norman hesitated for a moment before taking the seat opposite him. "I'll take whatever you're having," he said, gesturing vaguely to Danny's glass.

Danny nodded to the waitress, who disappeared to fetch the order. "Beautiful view, isn't it?" he said, gesturing to the ocean, where the sunset painted the horizon in hues of orange and pink.

Norman glanced out over the water, his expression skeptical. "I'm guessing you didn't bring me here to admire the view."

Danny chuckled, swirling the bourbon in his glass. "Straight to the point. I like that about you."

Norman leaned back in his chair, his eyes narrowing. "What can I do for you, Danny?"

Danny set his glass down and folded his hands on the table, his demeanor shifting from casual to businesslike. "I have an opportunity for you, Norman. One that could be... mutually beneficial."

Norman frowned. "Opportunity? I'm an insurance investigator, not a salesman."

Danny's smile didn't falter. "Please, hear me out first, then you could say yes or no."

Norman sighed, waving a hand for him to continue.

Danny leaned in slightly, his voice lowering. "You've been in this business a long time. Thirty years, give or take? An impeccable record, not a single black mark. You're the guy everyone trusts to sniff out fraud and protect the company's bottom line."

Norman's frown deepened. "Sounds like you've done some homework."

Danny's smile sharpened. "I have. You're nearing retirement and I'd wager you've seen enough people in your line of work leave with less than they deserve. Am I wrong?"

Norman stiffened, his jaw tightening. "You've done your homework again."

"Of course I have," Danny said smoothly. "You're meticulous, Norman. Methodical. You've earned your reputation, and you deserve to enjoy the fruits of your labor. But let's face it—pensions and savings only go so far."

Norman stared at him, his gaze unreadable. "You're awfully chatty for someone who hasn't told me why I'm here."

Danny reached into his pocket and pulled out a folded piece of paper, sliding it across the table. "Because I have a plan, and you're the key to making it work."

Norman picked it up and unfolded the paper, his eyes scanning the handwritten notes and figures. As the details sank in, his expression shifted from confusion to disbelief.

"You're talking about insurance fraud," Norman said, his voice low and dangerous.

Danny didn't flinch. "I'm talking about an opportunity."

Norman set the paper down, his gaze hard. "You must be out of your mind if you think I'd throw away my career for this."

Danny leaned back, completely unfazed. "I thought you might say that. But I'm not just asking you to risk everything for nothing. I'm offering you two million dollars."

Norman froze, the number hitting him like a freight train. For a moment, the noise of the bar seemed to fade, leaving only the pounding of his heartbeat in his ears.

"Two million dollars?" he repeated, his voice barely above a whisper.

Danny nodded. "Tax-free. Deposited into an offshore account I've already set up. It'll be untraceable, completely secure. All you have to do is help facilitate the claim once the accident happens."

Norman stared at him, his thoughts racing. "You're insane," he muttered.

"Am I?" Danny countered. "Think about it, Norman. You've spent three decades being the good guy, following the rules, protecting other people's money. Don't you think it's time to protect yourself for a change?"

Norman's hand tightened around his glass as he processed the offer. Two million dollars wasn't just tempting—it was life-changing.

"And if we get caught?" he asked finally.

Danny smiled. "We won't. The plan is airtight. A boating accident, shark infested water, no body, no evidence. I've covered every angle. And you—well, you're the golden boy. Who's going to suspect you?"

Norman's gaze drifted back to the paper, his mind warring between caution and greed. He knew he should walk away, call Danny's bluff and report him to the authorities.

But two million dollars... "I'll need time to think," he said at last, his voice gruff.

"Don't take too long," Danny replied smoothly, standing and buttoning his jacket. "Remember, Norman—opportunities like this don't come around every day."

Norman watched as Danny disappeared into the crowd, leaving the piece of paper on the table. He stared at it for a long moment before folding it neatly and tucking it into his pocket.

As the sun dipped below the horizon, the soft glow of the lights seemed almost mocking. Norman sipped his whiskey, the weight of the decision pressing down on him.

It was a risk. But was it worth it?

21. PLOT TO KILL

The Los Angeles skyline flickered through the penthouse windows, a glittering mirage against the night. The city pulsed beneath them—unaware, indifferent.

On the coffee table, a nautical map lay spread open, its edges curling slightly under the weight of a half-empty wine glass and a folded magazine. A photograph of a luxury yacht—sleek, white, Ocean Breeze printed in elegant script—rested beside it.

Lina stood at the window, her silk robe slipping from one shoulder, a cigarette smoldering between her fingers. Her reflection in the glass was calm, composed, but the wheels were turning.

She turned, walking toward the couch where Leslie sat stiffly, elbows resting on his knees, eyes locked on the map. He hadn't touched his drink.

She exhaled a ribbon of smoke, tapping the ash onto a crystal tray. "Danny will be driving the yacht himself," she murmured.

Leslie's brow furrowed. That was new.

"He knows boats," Lina continued, moving around the couch, curling onto the armrest beside him. "He has a license. He entertains clients all the time. It won't seem strange at all."

Leslie's fingers curled into fists. "And me?"

Her lips curved, dangerous and sweet. "You'll already be on board."

He stiffened. "Where?"

Lina reached out, tracing a delicate finger along his jawline. "Below deck. Hidden."

Leslie swallowed. "So, as far as Danny knows... it's just you and him?"

She smiled, tilting her head. "Exactly."

She leaned closer, her voice dropping to a whisper. "We'll be drinking. Celebrating. He'll be distracted. And when the moment is right, I will excuse myself to the bathroom. That's your cue. You come out of hiding."

Leslie's pulse thudded in his ears.

"You come up behind him, he'll be buzzed from drinking." Lina continued, her voice silk and steel. "He won't see you. He won't even have time to react. And then—"

She snapped her fingers.

Leslie exhaled sharply, staring down at the map. His eyes traced the red X drawn fifteen miles off the coast. Deep water. No land in sight.

"And after?" he asked, his voice barely above a whisper. Lina's fingers slid down his arm, her nails barely grazing his skin.

"After," she murmured, "I call the Coast Guard. I tell them Danny fell overboard. It was dark. The waves were high. I screamed, I turned the boat around, but..."

She let her hand fall as if brushing away a speck of dust.

Leslie's stomach twisted. It was airtight. Every detail accounted for.

Lina leaned in, her breath warm against his ear.

"Five million dollars, Leslie. No more ride shares. No more struggling. Just you and me, anywhere we want."

She kissed him—slow, deliberate, a promise and a poison all at once.

Leslie closed his eyes. And let himself believe it.

That Night

Leslie lay awake, staring at the ceiling.

The city thrived outside—sirens, laughter, the hum of a helicopter overhead—but none of it touched him.

His mind was already fifteen miles out. Already in the cold, black water. He turned onto his side, eyes drifting to Lina. She slept like a woman with nothing to fear.

Leslie sat up, rubbing his face. He could still walk away. He could disappear.

But then he thought about everything Lina had given him.

The car. The new apartment. The nights wrapped in silk sheets and whispered promises.

And he thought about Danny.

He saw him in the dark water. Arms thrashing. Calling his name.

A hand touched his arm. Leslie flinched.

"Can't sleep?" Lina's voice was thick with drowsiness.

He exhaled, shaking his head.

She sat up, brushing her hair back. The moonlight turned her eyes silver.

"It's going to be okay," she murmured, placing a hand on his cheek. "Once it's done... we're free."

Leslie swallowed hard. "I don't know if I can—"

Lina smiled. She had been waiting for him to say that. She leaned in, her lips brushing his ear.

"You can. Our stories will jibe."

Her fingers trailed down his chest, tracing slow patterns against his skin.

"Because you love me."

She kissed him again, deeper this time, and Leslie let himself drown in it.

Because maybe she was right. Maybe this was the only way.

22. THE REAL PLAN

Rebecca's bedroom was bathed in soft moonlight, the faint glow filtering through the gauzy curtains and casting long shadows across the unmade bed. The sheets were tangled, wrapped around Danny's legs as he lay back, his hands behind his head, staring at the ceiling with calm, calculating eyes.

Beside him, Rebecca propped herself up on one elbow, her dark hair falling in soft waves over her bare shoulder. She traced lazy circles on his chest with her finger, her voice teasing yet tinged with curiosity.

"You know," she murmured, her lips curving into a sly smile, "this would all be a lot easier if you didn't have a wife."

Danny chuckled, a low sound that barely broke the stillness of the room. His gaze didn't waver from the ceiling. "Not for long."

Rebecca's finger paused mid-circle, and she raised an eyebrow. "And you think Leslie's really going to go through with it?"

Turning his head to meet her gaze, Danny's smirk deepened. "He'll do it. Lina's already got him wrapped so tightly around her finger, the poor idiot probably thinks he's her knight in shining armor."

Rebecca shifted, sitting up slightly, her expression serious now. "You've told me bits and pieces, but I need to know exactly how this is going to play out. No surprises."

Danny exhaled, as if considering how much to share. Finally, he gestured vaguely toward the ceiling, his voice taking on a casual, almost rehearsed tone. "Alright. Here's how it works. Things go down next Thursday. Lina and I have been fighting for weeks, so we're going to 'make up.'" He air-quoted the words, his lips curling into a faint sneer.

Rebecca tilted her head, listening intently.

Danny continued, his voice steady, clinical. "We rent a yacht. Lina convinces Leslie to hide below deck. We'll sail miles offshore, close to sunset. Romantic, right? Perfect setup. Lina tells Leslie it's time, and he comes out of hiding and pushes me overboard when I'm not looking. Big splash, big panic. They race back to shore to call for help. Classic accident scenario."

Rebecca blinked, her brows knitting together. "And? How are you gonna get back to shore?"

"That's been arranged," Danny said, his smirk widening, "it'll be a recovery operation by the time the police determine I've 'disappeared' in that vast ocean, I'll be long gone. There's nothing to recover."

Rebecca leaned forward, resting her hand on his arm. "Is Lina in on the whole plan?"

Danny's smirk faded, replaced by a colder, more calculating look. "Almost, dear. She thinks she's orchestrating this to escape her miserable life and cash in on the insurance payout with me. But, I've got a better plan."

Rebecca sat back, her eyes widening. "What is it?"

Danny nodded, brushing a strand of hair from her face. "I'm gonna have to leave you hanging on that one. You'll know when it's time."

Rebecca's hand trembled slightly as she processed this. "Danny Carter, you'd better not keep anything important from me. I'm on your side, remember?" Rebecca said with seriousness.

"Of course not, you'll love the new plan when it's revealed." Danny said playfully.

"And Leslie? What happens to him when this all blows up?"

Danny shrugged, his expression icy. "Collateral damage. If anyone gets blamed, it's him. Lina will tell the police he was obsessed with her, and if the truth about the insurance fraud ever comes out, it'll all point to Leslie."

Rebecca frowned, her lips pressing into a tight line. "And the firm? What about James? They've hired a forensic accountant. They're sniffing around already."

Danny's smirk returned, his eyes gleaming. "Let them sniff. It'll take weeks for them to untangle the shell companies I set up. By the time they figure out I've been embezzling millions, the firm will collapse. James, everyone at the firm—will be too busy saving their own asses to come after you and I. You'll resign before it all comes crashing down. And then..."

He leaned in, brushing his lips against her ear. "We'll meet. Somewhere far away. Somewhere new."

Rebecca exhaled sharply, leaning back against the headboard. "You've really thought of everything."

Danny chuckled, lying back down beside her. "I always do."

They lay in silence for a moment, the weight of the plan hanging heavy in the air. Rebecca's fingers traced absent patterns on his arm, her mind racing.

Finally, she spoke, her voice barely above a whisper. "You'd better hope Lina doesn't find out you have other plans for her."

Danny's smirk didn't falter. "Trust me, she won't know what hit her. And that lovesick fool she's dragging along will take the fall for everything."

Rebecca stared at him, a flicker of unease crossing her face. "You're playing a dangerous game, Danny."

Danny closed his eyes, his smirk softening into something more self-satisfied. "Dangerous games are the only ones worth playing."

Rebecca rested her head against his chest, her thoughts churning. She trusted Danny—or at least she thought she did—but the enormity of the plan left her breathless. As his breathing steadied, hers remained shallow, her mind replaying his words over and over.

For a man who claimed to think of everything, she wondered if he'd truly accounted for every variable—or if his confidence would one day be his undoing.

23. FLASHBACK: THE BEGINNING OF BETRAYAL THREE YEARS EARLIER

Rebecca leaned against her desk, the dim light of her office lamp casting shadows across the walls. Her eyes followed Danny as he paced back and forth, his usual air of confidence replaced by a rare unease. The blinds were drawn, shutting out the world beyond the quiet office.

"You know," Rebecca began, her voice calm but pointed, "this would all be easier if you weren't dragging Lina along."

Danny stopped pacing, his hands shoved into his pockets. "Rebecca, she's my wife. What do you expect me to do? Just walk away?"

Rebecca tilted her head, a wry smile curving her lips. "I expect you to think about what's best for you. You've built this firm from the ground up. You've taken risks no one else would dare. And where's Lina in all this? Sitting at home, spending the money you work yourself to death for."

"She's not the problem," Danny shot back, though his voice lacked conviction.

Rebecca pushed off the desk and stepped closer, her heels clicking softly against the floor. "Isn't she?" she said, her tone softening as she reached out to touch his arm. "Danny, you deserve better. Someone who understands you. Someone who's been by your side through it all. Someone like me."

Danny's breath hitched, but he didn't pull away. For a moment, they stood in silence, the weight of her words hanging between them. Then Rebecca leaned in, her lips brushing against his.

It was tentative at first, but when he didn't move, she deepened the kiss. Her hands slid to his chest, pulling him closer.

When they finally broke apart, Danny looked away, his jaw tightening. "This... this isn't simple."

Rebecca smiled, her confidence unwavering. "It can be. You just have to stop letting her hold you back."

Later that night, Danny sat alone in his home office, the glow of his laptop illuminating the faint lines of tension on his face. The spreadsheet on the screen blurred together as Rebecca's words echoed in his mind.

"She's holding you back."

His eyes drifted to the framed photo on his desk—a picture of him and Lina on their wedding day. Her smile radiated joy, but all he felt now was exhaustion. He picked up the frame, his thumb brushing over the glass.

"I deserve better," he muttered under his breath before setting the photo face down on the desk.

24. THE ACCIDENT

The Pacific Ocean stretched endlessly, a vast sheet of darkening blue, gilded by the last golden light of the setting sun.

The Ocean Breeze, a sleek 45-foot luxury yacht, glided smoothly over the gentle swells, the rhythmic hum of its engine blending with the distant cries of seagulls. The Los Angeles coastline was nothing more than a faint blur in the distance, swallowed by haze. Fifteen miles offshore. Isolated. Private. A perfect place for an accident.

Danny Carter stood at the helm, one hand lazily gripping the wheel, the other wrapped around a tumbler of Macallan 18, the amber liquid sloshing faintly as the boat rocked. The breeze tousled his dark hair, his unbuttoned linen shirt rippling against his chest. He looked utterly at ease, exactly how Lina wanted him. Loose, buzzed, and unaware.

Jazz music purred through the yacht's speakers, mixing with the whisper of the waves. He smirked as he turned his gaze to Lina, who stood beside him, bathed in the warm hues of sunset. She lifted her champagne flute, her eyes meeting his with practiced affection.

"To us," she murmured, her voice smooth as silk. Danny chuckled, raising his glass. "To new beginnings."

They drank.

Lina watched the way he tilted his head back, the way his throat moved as he swallowed, the way his grip around the glass loosened slightly. Three drinks in. Tipsy, but not drunk. One more would do it.

She reached for the bottle chilling in the ice bucket, her fingers grazing his wrist as she poured him another. "We have the whole night ahead of us," she whispered. "Let's make it count."

Danny smirked, taking the glass, watching her over the rim as he sipped. His lips curled at the edges. "Damn, Lina. You trying to seduce me all over again?"

She laughed, stepping closer, pressing her palm lightly against his chest. "Maybe," she teased. "Maybe I just want to remind you what we had before everything got complicated."

Danny exhaled, shaking his head with a smile. "You always knew how to keep me on my toes."

Beneath deck, Leslie waited.

The small cabin was stifling, thick with the scent of polished teak and faint traces of gasoline. It felt like a coffin. The soft sway of the yacht did nothing to settle the tight knot in his stomach.

He could hear them. Lina's laughter. Danny's voice. The clink of glasses.

His fingers clenched into fists, damp with sweat. This was it.

His heartbeat pounded in his ears.

Then, the moment came.

Lina excused herself, slipping into the yacht's narrow hallway, her heels soft against the wooden floorboards.

Leslie saw her through the crack in the door.

She gave the signal. A quick, deliberate nod.

Leslie swallowed hard, pressed his hands against the cool wall, and stepped out of the shadows.

The Fall

Danny stood at the stern of the yacht, gazing out at the endless horizon, the glow of the sun dipping lower, setting the sky ablaze with deep oranges and bruised purples. His back was to the cabin door, one arm resting on the railing, his glass half-full.

He never heard Leslie approach from behind.

Leslie moved with purpose, his breath shallow, his heartbeat a drum pounding against his ribs. He took a step forward. Then another.

Danny exhaled, lifting his drink. "Hell of a view, huh, babe?"

Leslie lunged.

Both hands slammed into Danny's back with every ounce of strength he had.

Danny's glass slipped from his fingers, shattering against the deck in an explosion of crystal shards. His body pitched forward, arms flailing wildly, fingers scrambling for purchase.

He barely had time to suck in a breath before he hit the water.

A splash.

Silence.

Then—thrashing.

Danny surfaced, coughing, choking on saltwater as the ocean swallowed him. The current dragged him away from the yacht, his head bobbing wildly with each wave.

"LINA!" he screamed, his voice raw, carried by the wind. Leslie stood frozen, his hands still stretched forward, staring at the empty space where Danny had been just moments ago.

His pulse hammered. His chest heaved.

It was done.

But Danny was still alive. He was still screaming.

"LINA! YOU BASTARDS!"

Panic surged through Leslie's veins. He was supposed to sink. He was supposed to disappear.

Danny kept kicking, kept fighting, his arms slapping against the water as he tried to stay afloat. The waves tossed him farther and farther from the boat.

Lina was at Leslie's side in an instant, her fingers gripping his wrist like a vice.

"Drive."

Leslie's head snapped toward her, his breath ragged. "What?"

"DRIVE THE DAMN BOAT!" Lina hissed, her nails digging into his skin. "If we stay, he'll grab onto the ladder! We have to go—NOW!"

Leslie's fingers trembled as he stumbled back to the helm, his vision blurred, his mind screaming.

Danny's voice cut through the wind, desperate, furious.

"LINA! PLEASE! DON'T LEAVE ME!"

Leslie hesitated, his foot hovering over the throttle.

He turned to Lina, his expression wrecked. She met his gaze, steady, merciless.

Danny's voice changed then, the fear slipping away, replaced by pure rage.

"YOU THINK YOU CAN DO THIS TO ME?! I'LL KILL YOU BOTH!"

Leslie's jaw clenched.

Lina stepped behind him, her breath warm against his ear.

"Drive."

Leslie slammed the throttle forward.

The yacht roared to life, the engine growling as it surged ahead, leaving Danny's screams behind, swallowed by the waves. Lina watched him disappear, his outstretched arms the last thing visible before the ocean consumed him whole.

She exhaled, her shoulders relaxing, the tension bleeding from her body. "It's done," she murmured, almost to herself.

Leslie's hands clenched the wheel, his knuckles white.

"He was drunk. He slipped," Lina said softly, her voice laced with finality. "That's what happened."

Leslie said nothing.

His eyes remained fixed on the horizon, unable to look back.

Beneath the Surface

Danny kicked, fighting the frigid water, the salt burning his eyes, his limbs numb from adrenaline and exhaustion.

The yacht was gone.

But he wasn't alone.

His gaze darted around, searching, until he saw it—a small, dark silhouette bobbing just beyond the swells.

A waiting motorboat.

Danny pushed forward, swimming toward it, his chest heaving.

At the helm, Norman stood, cigarette between his lips. He smirked.

"Took your sweet time," he called as Danny grabbed onto the boat's side, gasping.

Danny hoisted himself up, collapsing onto the deck, his linen shirt soaked, clinging to him.

Norman chuckled, starting the engine. "And Lina?"

Danny grinned, slicking his wet hair back.

"She did well, he bought it."

Norman smirked, steering them into the darkness.

Danny leaned back, laughing softly. He grabbed a blanket that was prepared for him.

The perfect con.

25. LOST AT SEA

The ocean was a vast, dark expanse, especially restless and more sinister under a moonless night. The rhythmic crash of waves against the hull of the coast guard cutter filled the air, mingling with the distant thrum of helicopter blades slicing through the night sky. Searchlights skimmed across the water, illuminating rolling swells and empty darkness.

Aboard the lead search vessel, Lieutenant Gregson stood at the bow, his eyes scanning the waves through binoculars. The radio at his hip crackled.

"Negative visual. No sign of the man overboard."

Gregson exhaled sharply, lowering the binoculars. The ocean had a way of swallowing things—boats, bodies, secrets. But they had to keep looking.

Nearby, another officer leaned over the side, shining a powerful beam into the water. "If he's out there, he's not making it easy for us."

Above them, a police helicopter hovered, its searchlight cutting a glowing path across the surface.

"Still nothing," came the pilot's voice through Gregson's radio. "Current's strong tonight. If he went in where they said, he could be miles from here by now."

Back on shore, the pier was lined with patrol cars, their red and blue lights flashing against the black water. A small crowd had gathered—onlookers, reporters, and those with personal stakes in the search.

Detective Martin Morales stood among them, arms crossed, his gaze fixed on the horizon. His gut told him something was off. People drowned, yes. But men like Danny Carter didn't just vanish without a trace.

The early morning light cast a pale glow over the marina as police boats combed the waters just beyond the harbor. The once-still ocean was now alive with the hum of engines, the crackle of radios, and the occasional barked order from the lead investigator. Bright orange buoys marked the search zone, their presence stark against the endless blue.

Lina sat on a bench near the dock, wrapped in a blanket provided by one of the officers. Her makeup was smudged, her hair tousled, and her face pale and tear-streaked. She clutched a steaming cup of coffee in her trembling hands, though she didn't drink from it. Her gaze remained fixed on the horizon, as if willing Danny to reappear.

Leslie stood nearby, leaning against a lamppost, his posture rigid. His clothes were wrinkled from a sleepless night, and dark circles shadowed his eyes. He kept his arms crossed, as though physically holding himself together. His mind raced, replaying the events over and over again. The splash, the chaos, the moment he'd turned the yacht away under Lina's command.

What if the police didn't believe their story?

Detective Morales, a sharp-eyed man in his early fifties with a weathered face and a demeanor that demanded answers, approached them. His badge gleamed in the sunlight, clipped to his belt, and his notepad was already in hand. He stopped a few feet away, studying them both for a moment before speaking.

"Mrs. Carter," he began, his voice calm but firm. "I know this is a difficult time, but I need to ask you a few more questions about what happened yesterday."

Lina nodded, her lower lip trembling as she set the coffee cup down beside her. "Of course," she whispered, her voice hoarse. She dabbed at her eyes with a tissue, her hands shaking just enough to seem genuine.

Detective Morales crouched slightly to meet her gaze. "You said your husband slipped and hit his head before falling overboard. Can you walk me through what happened, step by step?"

Lina swallowed hard, casting a brief glance at Leslie before turning back to the detective. "We were celebrating," she began, her voice faltering. "Danny and I... we've had a rough couple of months, so he booked the yacht to make things right. It was supposed to be romantic. A fresh start."

Her voice broke, and she covered her mouth with her hand. Leslie watched, amazed at how seamlessly she slipped into the role of grieving wife. He knew it was all a performance, but even he felt a pang of sympathy.

"Take your time," Morales said gently, jotting notes in his pad.

Lina nodded, taking a shaky breath. "We stopped the boat to watch the sunset. Danny was leaning against the railing with his drink... and then he lost his balance. He slipped, hit his head on the edge, and fell into the water."

She sniffed, her tears flowing freely now. "Leslie and I... we tried to help.

I screamed for him to grab onto something, but he just... sank." She let out a sob, burying her face in her hands. "There was nothing we could do."

Morales nodded, his pen scratching against the notepad. "How far out were you when this happened?"

"Far," Lina said, her voice muffled. "At least fifteen miles from the marina. The current was so strong. It pulled him under almost immediately."

Morales turned to Leslie, his sharp eyes narrowing as he assessed the younger man. "Mr. Lai, you were at the helm. Is that correct?"

Leslie nodded, his throat dry. "Yeah. Lina... I mean, Mrs. Carter, asked me to come along with her."

"And you witnessed everything?"

"I did," Leslie replied, his voice unsteady. "I was steering the boat most of the time. When I heard Lina scream, I turned and saw Danny fall. I tried to stop him, but it all happened so fast." He rubbed the back of his neck, avoiding the detective's gaze. "I... I didn't know what to do."

Morales tilted his head slightly, his expression unreadable. "Why didn't either of you call for help immediately?"

Leslie hesitated, but Lina jumped in. "We tried!" she said, her voice rising in desperation. "But we were so far out, and the signal kept cutting out. By the time we got closer to shore, it was already too late."

Morales raised an eyebrow but said nothing, scribbling another note. "And you didn't see him resurface at all?"

Lina shook her head vehemently. "No. He just... disappeared. We stayed there and called out...

The detective straightened, tucking his notepad into his pocket. "Thank you both. We'll continue the search, but I have to be honest—the chances of finding him alive in these conditions are slim."

Lina let out a choked sob, covering her face again. Leslie reached out instinctively, placing a hand on her shoulder, though his own hands were trembling. "I'm so sorry," he murmured, the words hollow even to his own ears.

Morales watched them for a moment longer before stepping away, his expression neutral but his eyes sharp. He moved toward another officer, speaking in hushed tones as he gestured toward the search boats.

26. CRACKS IN THE FAÇADE

After the detective left, Lina stood abruptly, wrapping the blanket tighter around herself. "I need to go home," she said, her voice quiet but firm. She turned to Leslie, her red-rimmed eyes meeting his. "Can you take me?"

Leslie hesitated, glancing back at the water. The buoys bobbed in the distance, a silent reminder of what they'd left behind.

"Of course," he said, his voice barely above a whisper.

They walked to Leslie's car in silence, the weight of the morning pressing down on them. As Leslie started the engine, he cast a sideways glance at Lina. Her face was turned toward the window, her expression unreadable.

"You were... incredible back there," he said finally, his voice tentative. "With the detective, I mean. They believed you."

Lina turned to him slowly, a faint, bitter smile tugging at the corners of her lips. "They had to," she replied. "It's the truth, isn't it?"

Leslie nodded, though the knot in his stomach tightened. The truth was a slippery thing, and the longer he stayed by Lina's side, the harder it was to hold onto his own.

As they drove away from the marina, the first glimmers of doubt began to creep into Leslie's mind. Something about Lina's grief felt too perfect, too rehearsed. But he pushed the thought away, clinging to the hope that they'd done the right thing.

This is for their future.

27. HEADLINES AND CONDOLENCES

Lina sat curled up on the couch in the dimly lit living room, her hands trembling as she clutched a tissue. The muted sound of the TV filled the room, tuned to a local news channel. On the screen, a polished anchor delivered the grim headline:

"Tragedy at Sea: Prominent Accountant Danny Carter Presumed Dead After Boating Accident."

The anchor's voice was steady, professional, but the words pierced through the quiet like shards of glass.

"Authorities have called off the active search for Danny Carter, a senior partner at the prestigious firm Carter, Reid & Greene. According to his wife, Lina Carter, and their hired captain, Danny slipped and fell overboard during a private outing yesterday evening. Despite extensive efforts by law enforcement and Coast Guard teams, no body has been recovered."

Lina's lip quivered as she dabbed at her eyes, the tissue already soaked. The camera cut to a photo of Danny, smiling in a tailored suit, the perfect image of success. Below the picture, the words "Presumed Dead" appeared in bold.

The phone on the coffee table buzzed, pulling Lina from her trance. She sniffed, reaching for it and answering without looking at the caller ID.

"Hello?" she said, her voice raw and hoarse.

"Lina, it's Rebecca." The voice on the other end was soft, almost hesitant. "I just... I just heard the news. I'm so, so sorry."

Lina let out a shaky breath, her fingers tightening around the phone. "Thank you, Rebecca. It's been... it's been the hardest day of my life."

"I can't imagine," Rebecca replied, her tone laced with just the right amount of sympathy. "Danny was... he was such a force. I'm still in shock."

Lina closed her eyes, letting the words wash over her. "He was," she whispered. "I don't even know how to move forward."

Rebecca paused, as if searching for the right words. "If there's anything you need—anything at all—you call me. Don't hesitate."

"I will," Lina said, her voice cracking. "Thank you, Rebecca."

They exchanged a few more platitudes before the call ended. Lina set the phone down, staring at the screen as another name flashed across it: James Reid. She hesitated before answering.

"Lina," James said, his voice heavy with emotion. "I just heard. I... I don't even know what to say."

"Neither do I," Lina replied, her voice soft but steady. "It doesn't feel real."

James exhaled sharply, the sound of papers rustling in the background. "Danny was like a brother to me. I'm so sorry, Lina. If there's anything I can do—help with arrangements, paperwork, anything—please let me know."

"Thank you, James," Lina murmured. "I'll let you know." As the call ended, Lina sat back, letting the phone slip from her fingers. She stared at the flickering TV screen, her expression unreadable. After a moment, a small, almost imperceptible smile curled at the corners of her lips before she buried her face in her hands.

28. SHOCKWAVES AT THE FIRM

The offices of Carter, Reid & Greene were unusually quiet, the usual buzz of activity dampened by the somber news that had rippled through the company. Employees whispered in hushed tones, their expressions a mix of shock and disbelief. A framed photo of Danny sat on the reception desk, surrounded by a small bouquet of lilies and a candle flickering in his honor.

In James's office, he sat behind his desk, his head in his hands. The blinds were drawn, and the only light came from the dim glow of his computer screen. Rebecca sat across from him, her posture composed but her face carefully arranged into an expression of sadness.

"I can't believe it," James said, his voice thick with emotion. "Danny's gone."

Rebecca nodded, her gaze dropping to her lap. "It doesn't seem real. He was just here yesterday, talking about the new client portfolio."

James sighed, leaning back in his chair. "We've lost more than a partner, Rebecca. Danny was a pillar of this firm. His name is on the door, for God's sake."

"I know," Rebecca said softly. "It's... it's a huge loss."

James rubbed his temples, his frustration bleeding through. "We're already dealing with discrepancies in the books. Now this? How are we supposed to keep the firm afloat?"

Rebecca's eyes flickered briefly, but her tone remained calm. "We'll figure it out, James. We always do."

James shook his head, his mind racing. "I've been going through the financials all morning, trying to make sense of those transfers. Now I'm wondering... did Danny know something? Was he hiding something?"

Rebecca stiffened slightly, but she quickly masked her reaction with a shake of her head. "I don't think so. Danny would never..."

James frowned, his brow furrowing. "Wouldn't he? Lately, he's been distracted, leaving early, acting cagey. And now he's gone. It just doesn't sit right with me."

Rebecca leaned forward, her expression earnest. "James, I know this is overwhelming, but we can't jump to conclusions. Danny was under a lot of pressure, just like the rest of us. Maybe... maybe he just needed a break."

"A break?" James said bitterly, his voice rising. "Rebecca, he's most likely dead."

Rebecca winced, glancing toward the door as if worried someone might overhear. "I just mean... let's not rush to connect dots that aren't there."

James exhaled sharply, rubbing the bridge of his nose. "You're right. I'm sorry. I'm just... I'm grasping at straws here." Rebecca reached across the desk, placing a hand on his. "We'll get through this. Together."

James nodded reluctantly, his gaze distant. "We have to. For the firm."

As Rebecca stood to leave, her expression softened into one of quiet determination. But as soon as she stepped into the hallway, her mask cracked slightly. Her lips pressed into a thin line, her mind spinning with the weight of secrets she couldn't afford to let slip.

29. RUMORS AND LIES

Norman sipped his coffee, his gaze fixed on the small television in the corner of his cluttered office. Norman's expression remained calm, his sharp eyes betraying no emotion. The faint hum of the office around him—ringing phones, murmured conversations—seemed distant as he watched the news and the scrolling chyron announced: *Prominent Accountant Danny Carter Killed in Boat Accident.*

The door creaked open, and a colleague poked his head in. "Hey, Norm, you see this?"

Norman turned slightly, raising an eyebrow.

"Carter," the man continued, gesturing to the screen.

Norman nodded slowly, his lips twitching in the faintest hint of a smirk. "Yeah, terrible thing," he said, his tone measured. "But that's why they have people like us—to figure out what really happened."

The man gave a solemn nod. "Tragic, though. Guy had it all."

"Sure did," Norman replied, his smirk deepening as the door closed. Leaning back in his chair, he steepled his fingers, his mind already working through the next steps.

30. LIE LOW

Lina sat on the couch, the same one where she had planned Danny's "accident" with Leslie only days earlier. Now, she was the picture of grief, her silk robe wrapped tightly around her as the muted television replayed the news. Her phone buzzed on the coffee table, the vibrations slicing through the heavy silence.

She hesitated before picking it up, her hand trembling slightly. Leslie's name flashed on the screen.

"Leslie," she said, her voice soft and strained.

"Lina, it's all over the news," came his voice, frantic and breathless. "Everyone's talking about it. Are you okay?"

"I'm fine," she replied, closing her eyes briefly. "But Leslie, we need to lie low for a while. Don't call me unless it's absolutely necessary."

"Lina..."

"Listen to me," she snapped, her tone firm but laced with a practiced quiver. "We did what we had to do. There's no turning back now. The police will do their job, and as long as we stay calm, no one will suspect a thing."

Leslie hesitated, his silence stretching uncomfortably.

"Do you understand?" Lina pressed, her voice softening slightly.

"Yeah," he said finally, though the doubt in his tone was unmistakable. "Yeah, okay."

She hung up and leaned back against the cushions, exhaling deeply. For a brief moment, a faint glimmer of satisfaction crossed her face. Everything was going according to plan—for now.

31. AFTERMATH

James sat at his desk, his head in his hands, the chaos of the morning swirling around him. The firm's phones hadn't stopped ringing since news of Danny's death broke. Clients were demanding answers, colleagues whispered nervously in the hallways, and the weight of it all was crushing.

Rebecca walked in, balancing two steaming cups of coffee. Her heels clicked softly against the polished floor as she set one cup in front of him.

"Here," she said gently. "You look like you need this." James nodded gratefully, taking a long sip. "This is just... unbelievable," he muttered, staring at his computer screen.

Rebecca sat across from him, cradling her own cup. "It doesn't feel real," she said, her tone carefully measured. "How could something like this happen to someone like Danny? He was always so careful... so in control."

James shook his head, his expression darkening. "This is going to leave a huge hole in the firm. His clients, his accounts— it's a mess. And the timing... Rebecca, it couldn't be worse."

Rebecca offered a sympathetic smile, though her eyes gleamed with something more calculating. "We'll figure it out, James. We always do."

Rebecca and James sat in the sleek conference room, joined by Michael Langston, the forensic accountant hired to investigate the firm's financial discrepancies.

The table was littered with files and spreadsheets, each one marked with colorful tabs and highlighter streaks.

Michael leaned forward, his expression grim as he pointed to a section of a document. "Here's where we're at," he began, his voice deliberate. "I've installed an AI tool to search for anomalies and it traced the missing funds to multiple offshore accounts, but I can't determine exactly who's behind the transfers. Whoever did this knew what they were doing. It's sophisticated, and they covered their tracks well."

James frowned, leaning closer. "But you've found something, right? Anything concrete?"

Michael hesitated, tapping his pen against the table. "Nothing definitive. The transfers were routed through shell corporations, and all the accounts are under generic business names. It's going to take time to untangle it. Even for AI."

Rebecca crossed her arms, her expression tense. "Time isn't something we have," she said sharply. "If the clients catch wind of this, we're done."

Michael spread his hands in an apologetic gesture. "I'm doing everything I can, but this feels like an inside job, someone with intimate knowledge of the firm's systems."

James exchanged a glance with Rebecca, his jaw tightening.

"An inside job..." he repeated, his voice heavy with suspicion.

Rebecca's lips pressed into a thin line. "Well," she said slowly, "there's only a handful of people who would have that kind of access. And one of them is... gone now."

James stiffened, her words sinking in like a lead weight. "You think Danny was involved?" he asked, his voice barely above a whisper.

Rebecca hesitated, then shrugged, feigning reluctance. "I don't know, James. But we can't ignore the possibility."

Michael cleared his throat. "I'll need full access to all financial records—past and present, if you want me to keep digging. If there's something to find, I'll find it. Well, AI will find it."

James hesitated, his mind racing. Finally, he nodded. "Do whatever you have to do."

Rebecca is definitely alarmed, but she keeps her composure. Things have to move along faster now, otherwise paper is not going to wrap fire.

32. THE FUNERAL WITHOUT A BODY

The cemetery was quiet, save for the soft rustle of leaves in the midday breeze. A modest crowd gathered under a white canopy, their faces etched with grief and solemnity. Beneath the canopy stood a simple black memorial plaque, its polished surface engraved with the words:

In Loving Memory of Daniel Carter

1975 – 2024

Next to the plaque, a framed photograph of Danny smiled back at the mourners. His confident expression seemed almost mocking in its perfection, a cruel reminder of the life cut short. A floral arrangement of white lilies and roses encircled the memorial, their fragrant presence clashing with the stark reality of a funeral without a casket.

The priest stood at the front, his hands clasped in reverence. His deep, measured voice carried over the mourners, each word steeped in somber reflection.

"Today, we gather to celebrate the life of Daniel Carter," he began. "A husband, a colleague, and a man whose life was

135

tragically cut short. Though we are left without his physical remains, his spirit lives on in our memories and in the lives he touched."

Heads bowed across the crowd, and a faint murmur of agreement rippled through the mourners. Some dabbed their eyes with tissues, their sorrow palpable. Among them stood James and Rebecca, their dark suits crisp and formal. James's face was lined with genuine grief, his brow furrowed as he stared at the plaque.

Beside him, Rebecca appeared calm and composed, her dark eyes sharp and assessing, taking in every detail of the event.

Lina sat in the front row, the widow in mourning. Her black veil shrouded her face, concealing all but the faint quiver of her lips as she dabbed at her eyes with a handkerchief. To anyone watching, she was the very picture of a grieving wife, her movements calculated yet convincing.

But behind the veil, her thoughts raced.

It's all coming together, Lina thought, her heart pounding. *I just need to wait a little longer. No sudden moves. No mistakes.*

For a brief moment, her eyes flicked toward the empty rows at the back of the gathering, where Leslie should have been. His absence didn't surprise her—she'd instructed him to stay away—but it unsettled her nonetheless. She knew he was unraveling, his guilt gnawing at him like a wound that refused to heal. She needed him to hold it together, at least for a little while longer.

136

The priest concluded his sermon with a prayer, and the crowd murmured their Amens. One by one, the mourners approached the plaque, laying down flowers or pausing to reflect before retreating to the parking lot.

Lina lingered near her car in the cemetery parking lot, her veil pushed back now that most of the crowd had dispersed. The afternoon sun glinted off the polished black paint of her sedan, casting long shadows across the gravel.

James approached her cautiously, his hands tucked into the pockets of his coat. "Lina," he said softly, "I just wanted to say how sorry I am. If there's anything you need, don't hesitate to reach out."

Lina nodded, her voice trembling with carefully rehearsed emotion. "Thank you, James. It's been... hard."

James hesitated, his eyes searching hers for a moment before he gave her a tight smile and stepped away. Rebecca was waiting for him near their car, watching Lina with a curious expression.

After James left, Rebecca approached, her heels clicking softly against the gravel. "Lina," she began, her voice gentle but probing. "You're holding up remarkably well. I don't know how you're doing it."

Lina offered a faint, sad smile. "I have no choice," she replied. "I have to be strong. For Danny."

Rebecca's gaze lingered on her for a moment longer, a flicker of something unreadable crossing her face. Then she nodded, murmured a polite goodbye, and walked away.

137

Lina exhaled softly, her fingers tightening on her car keys. From across the lot, she caught sight of Norman Fields leaning casually against his car. His dark sunglasses concealed his sharp eyes, but Lina could feel his gaze on her.

Norman checked his phone briefly, a faint smirk tugging at the corner of his mouth before he slipped the device back into his pocket. He gave Lina a curt nod, then climbed into his car and drove off.

Lina sat in the driver's seat of her own car, her hands gripping the steering wheel tightly. The weight of the day pressed down on her, and for the first time, her composure began to crack. She exhaled shakily, her breath fogging the air.

Reaching into her purse, she pulled out a compact mirror and flipped it open. Her reflection stared back, weary but resolute. She dabbed at her face with a tissue, careful not to smudge her makeup.

Her mind wandered briefly to Leslie, picturing him in their apartment, pacing the floor, wracked with guilt. She couldn't afford for him to fall apart now—not when they were so close.

"It's almost over," she whispered to herself, her voice steady despite the tremble in her hands. "Just a little longer."

She closed the compact with a soft click, started the engine, and drove away from the cemetery, leaving the hollow ritual behind.

33. HIDDEN IN PARADISE

The sun cast a warm golden glow over the turquoise waters of the Adriatic Sea, the gentle waves lapping against the shore just beyond the veranda of Danny Carter's villa. The sprawling oceanfront property was the epitome of luxury—white walls, sleek modern furnishings, and open spaces that let the sea breeze flow freely through the house.

Danny reclined on a plush chaise lounge, a glass of aged whiskey in his hand and a satisfied smirk on his face. Dressed in a loose linen shirt and tailored shorts, he looked like a man who had left his worries far behind.

But appearances were deceiving.

The phone beside him buzzed, its encrypted app displaying a single name: R. Danny picked it up, took another sip of his whiskey, and accepted the call.

"Rebecca," he said smoothly, his voice carrying the faintest edge of annoyance.

"Danny," Rebecca's voice came through, clipped and urgent. "Do you have any idea how hard it is to keep James off our trail? He's getting closer every day. This Michael guy installed an AI tool to help him find the truth. I don't know how much longer I can stall him."

Danny chuckled softly, leaning back further into the lounge. "You're doing fine, Rebecca. James is thorough, but he's not invincible. Just keep feeding him and this Michael guy dead ends and tying him up in procedural nonsense. He'll burn out eventually."

Rebecca wasn't amused. "That might work for a little while, but it's not going to last forever.

Michael's still digging, and they've already flagged some of the transfers. It's only a matter of time before they realize everything points back to you."

Danny swirled his drink, watching the ice clink softly against the glass. "Let them dig," he said calmly. "They'll come up with nothing concrete. And by the time they do, this whole thing will have blown over. Besides, once the insurance pays out, I'll be long gone. So will you."

Rebecca hesitated, her voice dropping slightly. "And where exactly are you, Danny? I mean, you've got this whole thing under control, but you won't even tell me where you are."

Danny's smirk faded, his tone turning cold. "You know why I can't tell you. It's safer for both of us if my location stays a secret. Loose lips sink ships, Rebecca."

"I'm not some loose-lipped amateur," she snapped, her frustration bubbling to the surface. "I've risked everything to help you. The least you can do is trust me."

Danny sighed, rubbing his temple with his free hand. "I do trust you, Rebecca. But trust doesn't mean being careless. When the time is ripe, I'll tell you everything. For now, just focus on keeping James, Michael, and his AI busy. Can you do that?"

Rebecca exhaled sharply. "Fine. But this double indemnity claim needs to move forward. Lina's been lying low, but she has to file soon."

"I know," Danny said. He stood, walking toward the edge of the veranda, where the waves glimmered under the afternoon sun.

"I'll contact her soon and give her the green light. As far as she knows, everything is going according to plan."

Rebecca's voice softened, though her frustration lingered. "And Norman? He's still on board?"

Danny smiled faintly. "Norman's playing his part perfectly. Once Lina files the claim, he'll grease the wheels to make sure it's approved. He knows better than to screw this up."

There was a pause on the line before Rebecca spoke again. "Danny... what happens after Lina realizes she's not the beneficiary? She's not going to take that well."

Danny's smirk returned, cruel and calculating. "By the time she figures it out, it'll be too late. She'll try to go after Leslie, throw him under the bus, but it won't matter. The money will already be in the trust, under your control. Lina's nothing more than a pawn, Rebecca. Don't waste your sympathy on her."

141

Rebecca didn't respond immediately, but Danny could hear her exhale, long and slow. "I just hope you're right. If this blows up in our faces—"

"It won't," Danny cut in sharply. "Stick to the plan. Keep your head down, keep James guessing, and everything will be fine."

That evening, Danny sat at a sleek desk in his villa, the room illuminated by the soft glow of a lamp. He logged into his secure communication app and typed out a brief message to Lina: "It's time. File the claim. Everything's ready."

He leaned back in his chair, letting out a long breath. The pieces were falling into place, just as he had envisioned.

Lina would play her role, Leslie would continue to flounder in guilt, and Rebecca would keep the firm's investigation bogged down in red tape.

As for Norman, Danny had no doubt the insurance investigator would smooth over any potential hurdles. Norman had enormous reasons for ensuring this scheme succeeded, and Danny had made sure those reasons were compelling enough.

He glanced at the phone, his thoughts drifting briefly to Lina. He could almost picture her reaction when she realized she had been cut out of the deal, her anger simmering beneath her carefully crafted mask of grief. It would be satisfying to watch her unravel. "Almost there," Danny murmured to himself, staring out at the ocean. "Just a little longer."

In the distance, the waves rolled endlessly against the shore, their steady rhythm a stark contrast to the web of lies and deceit that had brought him to this secluded paradise. Two sexy strippers came out of the bathroom naked. One of them turned on the music and both started dancing and giving Danny a lap dance.

For now, he was safe. For now, the plan was working. But even Danny, in all his confidence, couldn't shake the faintest flicker of unease—a whisper in the back of his mind that the best-laid plans rarely went off without a hitch.

34. DOUBLE INDEMNITY

Lina sat across from the claims officer in the pristine, sterile office. The air conditioning hummed faintly, doing little to ease the tension radiating from her as she clasped her hands tightly in her lap.

Dressed in an impeccably tailored black suit, Lina exuded elegance and control, though a faint tremor in her fingers betrayed her unease.

The claims officer, a woman with a practiced air of sympathy, flipped through the thick policy file marked *Daniel Carter – Double Indemnity*. A framed photograph of her family on the desk lent a human touch to her otherwise clinical demeanor. She glanced up at Lina, offering a polite smile.

"Mrs. Carter, thank you for coming in," the officer began, her voice warm but professional. "I'm so sorry for your loss."

"Thank you," Lina replied smoothly, though the words felt hollow in her mouth. "It's been... difficult."

The officer nodded, closing the file. "Your claim is under review, but I need to inform you—there seems to be an issue with the policy."

Lina's breath hitched, but she kept her face neutral. "An issue? What kind of issue?"

The claims officer maintained her well-practiced composure, folding her hands atop the file. "I don't have all the details, Mrs. Carter, but our senior investigator, Mr. Norman Fields, has been assigned to the case. He'll be in touch with you very soon."

Lina's grip on her handbag tightened, though her expression remained calm. "How soon can I expect to hear from him?"

"Within the next few days," the officer replied. "Thank you for your patience, Mrs. Carter."

Lina rose gracefully, forcing a polite nod. "Of course. Thank you."

Her heels clicked sharply against the tiled floor as she exited the office, the sound echoing faintly in the sterile space.

Once inside her car, Lina's mask of composure shattered. She gripped the steering wheel so tightly her knuckles turned white, her jaw clenched as she fought to steady her breathing.

What the hell is going on?

She reached into her handbag for her phone, intending to call Leslie, Norman—*anyone*. But after a moment, she stopped, taking a shaky breath and forcing herself to think clearly.

"Stay calm," she whispered aloud. "Stick to the plan." Her pulse still raced, but she shoved the phone back into her bag, started the engine, and pulled out of the parking lot with calculated precision.

145

Two Days Later.

The chime of the doorbell echoed through the opulent halls of Lina's mansion. The late morning sun streamed through the large windows, illuminating the marble floors and ornate furnishings.

Lina strode to the door, her expression calm but her heart pounding. She had been waiting for this moment, alternating between dread and determination. Pulling the door open, she was met with the cool, composed figure of Norman Fields.

"Mrs. Carter," he greeted her with a polite nod, his leather briefcase in one hand. "Thank you for agreeing to meet."

"Let's just get to the point," Lina replied, stepping aside to let him in. Her tone was clipped, betraying her growing impatience.

Norman entered, his sharp eyes taking in the lavish interior before setting his briefcase on the living room table. He clicked it open with practiced ease and pulled out a slim folder.

"There's been a significant update to the policy," Norman said, sliding the folder across the table toward her.

Lina crossed her arms, her calm exterior beginning to crack. "What kind of update?"

Norman opened the folder, tapping a document inside. "The beneficiary was changed shortly before Mr. Carter's accident. You're no longer listed as the recipient."

For a moment, Lina didn't comprehend the words. Then, like a hammer blow, they hit her full force.

"That's impossible," she said, her voice rising. "I was the beneficiary. Danny told me—"

Norman remained unflappable, closing the folder with a crisp snap. "I can assure you the change is legitimate. The new beneficiary is legally binding."

Lina's shock turned to fury. Her nails dug into the armrest of the chair as her mind raced.

"Who?" she demanded. "Who's the new beneficiary?"

Norman offered a faint smile, unreadable behind his professional demeanor. "I'm afraid I can't disclose that information. Privacy laws prevent me from sharing the name."

Lina's composure shattered completely. She stood abruptly, her voice trembling with anger. "You expect me to just accept this? I was his wife!"

Norman rose slowly, collecting his briefcase. "I understand this is difficult, Mrs. Carter. If you have further questions, I suggest consulting your legal counsel."

With that, he turned and walked to the door. "Good day, Mrs. Carter," he said over his shoulder before letting himself out.

The door clicked shut, leaving Lina standing frozen in the middle of the living room. For a moment, her mind went blank, her thoughts paralyzed by the enormity of the betrayal.

Then, like a dam breaking, the fury poured out. She grabbed the nearest wine glass from the table and hurled it across the room. It shattered against the wall, shards raining onto the marble floor.

Breathing heavily, she reached for her phone with shaking hands. Her mind raced as she opened her messages, her fingers hovering over the keyboard.

Danny, you bastard. You lied to me. YOU LIED.

She deleted the words before sending them, throwing the phone onto the couch in frustration. Her chest heaved as the truth sank in—Danny had played her for a fool. All her careful planning, her manipulations, her sacrifices... all for nothing.

She clenched her fists, her nails digging into her palms. "This isn't over," she whispered to herself, her voice cold and venomous. "Not by a long shot."

As she paced the room, her mind began to churn with plans for revenge. Whatever Danny had done, whoever he had chosen over her—it wouldn't matter in the end. She would make sure of it.

35. THE BETRAYAL UNVEILED

Lina stood motionless, her chest heaving as the echo of the impact faded into the silence of the mansion's grand living room. For a moment, she simply stared at the mess, her mind racing.

Then, snapping out of her daze, she grabbed her phone from the table, her fingers trembling as she typed a message.

"We need to talk. Now!"

The abandoned warehouse loomed in the darkness, its corrugated metal walls reflecting the pale glow of a faulty streetlight. Crickets chirped in the night, the eerie stillness broken only by the occasional shuffle of Leslie's pacing feet.

He leaned against the hood of his Mustang, his face pale and drawn, his burner phone clenched tightly in one hand. Every sound—the rustle of wind, the distant hum of a passing car—made him flinch. He glanced at his phone again, cursing under his breath.

When Lina's car finally pulled into the lot, its headlights cutting through the shadows, Leslie straightened, his heart pounding. She stepped out, her trench coat swaying slightly in the breeze. Her face was cold, her eyes sharp as she approached.

"What the hell is this about, Lina?" Leslie demanded, his voice rising with barely contained frustration. "I thought you said we were gonna lie low."

Lina stopped a few feet from him, her arms crossed tightly over her chest. "Something unexpected happened."

Leslie frowned, his nerves already frayed. "What's going on? Did you file the claim?"

Lina's jaw tightened. For a long moment, she said nothing, her piercing gaze making Leslie squirm. Then she finally spoke.

"There's no claim to file," she said, her voice flat.

Leslie blinked, confusion spreading across his face. "What do you mean?"

Lina's lips pressed into a thin line. "I'm not the beneficiary anymore, Leslie."

The words hung in the air, cold and heavy. Leslie's face contorted in disbelief, his breath catching in his throat.

"What?" he stammered. "That's impossible. You're his wife! Who else could it be?"

Lina took a sharp breath, her tone biting. "Norman Fields came to see me, the insurance investigator. He told me to my face. He had the paperwork to back it up."

Leslie's voice rose, panic creeping into his tone. "He just came to your house and *dropped that* on you?"

"That's right," Lina snapped. "And when I pressed him for details, he said he couldn't disclose who the new beneficiary is."

Leslie's pacing quickened, his hands tugging at his hair. "This can't be happening. No, no, this—this doesn't make sense!"

"Oh, it makes perfect sense," Lina said, her voice icy. "We've been played."

Leslie stopped pacing, his eyes wide with realization. He pointed a trembling finger at her. "Oh my God. I knew this was a bad idea. I *knew it*! We killed a guy for nothing, Lina. Nothing! I believed you!"

For a fleeting moment, Lina's expression softened, but the cold calculation returned almost instantly.

"Well, believe this now: Danny cut me out completely."

Leslie's bitter laugh echoed in the empty lot. "Yeah, no shit!"

"And now what? What the hell are we supposed to do now? Just sit here, broke, waiting for the cops to show up?"

Lina's eyes narrowed, her voice low and firm. "I'm not sitting here waiting for anything."

Leslie barked a harsh laugh. "Oh yeah? And what's your brilliant plan?"

Lina straightened, her voice cold and unwavering. "We find out who's behind this. We figure out who the new beneficiary is and we make them talk."

Leslie's laughter turned bitter. "What good would that do? The money's gone, Lina. We can't get our hands on it anymore!"

Suddenly, he grabbed her by the shoulders, shaking her slightly.

"Lina, listen to me. Sell the house. At least that should be yours. We need to skip town before the cops figure things out!"

Lina yanked herself free, her eyes blazing. "Will you get a hold of yourself?" she snapped.

She stepped away, pacing in a tight circle as she spoke. "We have to get to the bottom of this."

Leslie exhaled shakily, his hands falling to his sides. "This is all so... so fucked up."

Lina stopped, her expression hardening with a new determination. "Norman."

Leslie's head snapped up, his brows knitting in confusion. "What about him?"

"Think about it," Lina said, her voice measured. "He's been on this policy for years. He's handling the claim. If anyone knows what Danny's been up to, it's him."

Leslie stared at her, the color draining from his face. "Are you even listening to yourself? You just told me he wouldn't divulge any information. How the hell are you gonna find out?"

"Oh, I'll find a way," Lina said with determination.

He wanted to argue, to demand a way out of this mess, but deep down, he knew this whole thing just fell off the cliff. But what Leslie didn't know was that he has been a pawn, a scapegoat all this time and Lina hasn't chosen to tell him. She never intended to walk into the sunset with Leslie, but now the situation has dramatically and shockingly changed.

152

The weight of their uneasy alliance settled between them, heavy and unspoken. The only way forward was together, no matter how treacherous the path might be.

36. THE IRON CAGE

Lina burst through the front door, her steps frantic. She didn't stop to close it behind her. She couldn't. Her breath came in short, ragged gasps as she bolted up the grand staircase, gripping the railing to keep herself steady.

She reached the bedroom, shoving the door open with such force that it slammed against the wall. The echo rang through the mansion, but she barely heard it. Her focus was singular.

The closet.

Lina tore through the huge walk-in bedroom closet like a woman possessed. Silk blouse and designer dresses, once arranged meticulously, now lay in a heap on the floor. The safe was in the back, behind a row of neatly hung coats. She yanked them aside, her breathing shallow, her pulse hammering.

She punched in the code. 1-8-9-4. Danny's and her birthdays combined. The lock beeped, and the heavy door creaked open.

Inside, stacks of neatly arranged documents sat beside one bundle of cash and Danny's collection of rare watches. But

Lina's eyes locked onto one envelope—PRENUPTIAL AGREEMENT—bold and clinical in all caps.

Her fingers trembled as she pulled it out. Even though there are only a few pages, the legal jargon was nevertheless heavy. She had signed it many years ago, young and blinded by love. She never imagined she'd need to read it again.

She sat on the edge of the bed, the dim glow of the bedside lamp casting long shadows. Her eyes skimmed over the opening paragraphs, the stiff legalese blurring together. It was just words—until it wasn't.

In the event of dissolution of marriage, the undersigned, Lina Wilkins, soon to be Lina Carter, acknowledges that she shall not be entitled to any ownership interest in the marital home and all things inside and outside the home or all other assets before and after the marriage. Personal properties such as clothing, jewelry, handbags, and shoes can be exempted.

Her breath hitched.

She read it again.

And again.

Not entitled to the house. Not entitled to anything.

The words felt like a knockout punch. Her vision swam.

Furthermore, after a period of ten (10) years, should the marriage terminate for any reason, except in the case of infidelity,the undersigned shall receive a financial settlement of one million U.S. dollars.

One million. That was it. That was all she would have gotten if she left him. Chances were, she wouldn't be getting that one million dollars either. She had an extramarital affair with Leslie which Danny put her up to it so that to ensure Leslie's involvement in his scam! Danny thought of everything.

The house. The investments. The properties. Virtually all of it would remain Danny's.

Lina pressed a shaking hand to her forehead. Who the hell would sign a prenuptial like that?! But, she had been so young when she married him. A 22-year-old who thought she had won the lottery—an older, successful husband, a life of luxury. She never thought to question anything.

Danny had told her it was just a formality—that every rich man had one, that it didn't mean anything. She had laughed, signed it, and never looked back. Why would she? Danny was her future, her protector, her permanent meal ticket.

Now, he was gone.

And she was left with nothing.

Lina's hands clenched the edges of the paper, the crisp pages crumpling under her grip. No house. No empire. No fallback. Danny had planned for everything—even if their marriage failed, he had made sure she'd never take him for a cent more than he allowed.

And now, he had taken it all.

A strangled sound escaped her throat—a mixture of laughter and something dangerously close to a sob.

She had played along with Danny's game. Helped him fake his death. Betrayed Leslie. And for what?

A cruel, empty mansion she couldn't even sell.

Her fingers curled around the paper, crumpling it. She wanted to tear it apart, to shred it to pieces. But she didn't. She forced herself to breathe, to think.

Danny had outplayed her at every turn. But the game wasn't over yet.

She swallowed the lump in her throat, smoothed out the paper, and slipped it back into the folder. Then, with a cold determination settling in her bones, she placed it back inside the safe and shut the door.

Lina Carter had been used. Tossed aside like an old dress that no longer fit.

But she wasn't going to let this be the end of her story.

Not yet.

37. THE FINAL LOOSE ENDS

The secure phone buzzed on Norman Fields' desk, its soft vibration echoing in the dimly lit room. He glanced at the encrypted messaging app that blinked on the screen: Call incoming – Daniel Carter.

Norman leaned back in his chair, adjusting his glasses as he tapped the answer button. The video feed blinked to life, revealing Danny sitting in a sleek, minimalist hotel room. The distant hum of an air conditioner and faint chatter from a nearby market hinted at his location, somewhere far from home.

"Norman," Danny said, his voice crisp and businesslike. "How's everything on your end?"

Norman adjusted the angle of his phone to block out the cluttered desk behind him. "Moving along," he replied. "The insurance company's waiting on my final report. I've told them I'm waiting for the police to officially close their investigation. That should help with the payout approval a lot."

Danny nodded, his expression unreadable. "And the police? Any issues there?"

"No," Norman said. "They're treating it as an accident, just as we planned. The report should come out in a week, and once it's official, I can wrap up my findings. The payout will follow soon after."

"Good," Danny said, leaning back in his chair. "Everything's falling into place."

Norman hesitated, his fingers drumming lightly on the desk. "Not everything," he said finally.

Danny's eyes narrowed. "Leslie."

Norman nodded. "He's a problem, Danny. The guy's barely holding it together. I've seen it before—nervous types like him don't last long under pressure. Sooner or later, he'll crack, and when he does, everything we've worked for could come crashing down."

Danny exhaled sharply, rubbing a hand over his jaw. "I figured this might happen," he muttered. "Lina was supposed to keep him in line, but clearly, that's not enough."

Norman leaned forward, his voice lowering. "It's not just about keeping him in line. He knows too much, Danny. The boating accident, the insurance claim, all of it. If the cops pick him up, it won't take much for him to spill everything."

Danny's gaze hardened, his tone turning icy. "Then we deal with him."

Norman's lips pressed into a thin line. "And by 'deal with him,' I assume you mean permanently?"

Danny nodded, his expression unflinching. "There's no other option. He's a liability we can't afford to keep around."

159

Norman leaned back, letting out a slow breath. "I was afraid you'd say that."

"You disagree?" Danny asked, his tone sharp.

"No," Norman said quickly. "I agree he's a problem. But this isn't a simple cleanup job, Danny. Leslie isn't some lowlife off the street. He's emotionally unstable, yes, but he's also desperate. That makes him dangerous. If we're going to do this, we need to be absolutely certain there's no trail leading back to us."

Danny's eyes narrowed, his mind clearly racing. "What are you suggesting?"

Norman hesitated, then spoke with deliberate care. "I need to bring in someone I trust to take care of it."

Danny tilted his head, studying Norman through the screen. "Do you have someone in mind?"

"I do," Norman said. "But it'll cost extra."

Danny smirked faintly. "How much extra?"

"Forty," Norman replied without hesitation.

Danny leaned back, considering the amount. "Fine. I'll transfer the money to the account we set up. But it has to be clean, Norman. No loose ends."

Norman nodded. "You know me, Danny. I don't leave loose ends."

Danny's expression softened slightly, though his voice remained cold. "Good. Once Leslie's out of the picture, we can move on to the next phase. Rebecca's handling things on her end, and once the money's in the account, it's just a matter of staying quiet until this all blows over."

Norman leaned forward, his tone firm. "And what about Lina?"

Danny's smirk widened into something more sinister. "Lina's no different from Leslie—just another pawn. Let her stew for a while. She's harmless without the money."

Norman's lips twitched, but he didn't comment. He knew better than to question Danny's ruthlessness.

"I'll update you when it's done," Norman said, his voice steady.

"Make sure you do," Danny replied. "And, Norman? Be careful."

Norman nodded, ending the call. The screen went dark, leaving him alone with his thoughts. He stared at the blank display for a moment, then leaned back, exhaling slowly.

Pulling open the drawer of his desk, Norman retrieved a burner phone. He scrolled through the contacts until he found the name he was looking for.

His thumb hovered over the call button for a moment before he pressed it. The phone rang twice before a gruff voice answered.

"Señor Duele," Norman said, his voice calm and professional. "I have a job for you."

38. THE CONFESSION

The Venice Beach boardwalk was quieter at night, stripped of the usual chaos—no street performers, no tourists, no overpriced sunglasses stands hawking knockoffs under neon lights. Just the restless crash of waves and the occasional murmur of a late-night wanderer.

Rebecca walked along the sand, her heels sinking slightly with each step. She spotted Norman sitting on a bench near the graffiti-covered remains of an old concrete skate ramp, his trench coat pulled tight against the ocean breeze. He was nursing a cigarette instead of a drink, the ember glowing faintly in the dark.

She stopped a few feet away, studying him. "Didn't peg you for the Venice Beach type."

Norman smirked, exhaling smoke. "I'm not. But I figured this place doesn't have as many cameras as a damn hotel lounge."

Rebecca took the unspoken meaning. This was the kind of place where deals went down, where things got said and then forgotten.

162

She pulled her jacket tighter around herself and sat beside him, the scent of salt and cigarette smoke mixing in the air.

There was a beat of silence. Just the tide rolling in.

"I want to hear it from you," Rebecca said finally. "The rescue."

Norman let out a short, quiet chuckle. "Danny didn't give you the grand retelling?"

"I trust details, not stories," she said, her gaze steady.

Norman flicked the cigarette into the sand, watching the ember die. "Fine. I took a smaller boat out before everything was gonna go down, anchored past visibility range. Kept low, stayed patient. The yacht came into view exactly when it was supposed to."

He paused, then smirked slightly. "Leslie did his part. Clumsy, but he did it. Danny hit the water right on cue. Maybe a little too well—he really sold the struggle."

Rebecca tilted her head. "And then?"

Norman leaned back against the bench, watching the waves. "I moved in. Hauled him out fast. He was soaked, coughing up seawater, pissed off. You'd think a guy who planned his own drowning wouldn't complain about getting wet."

Rebecca exhaled through her nose—almost a laugh, but not quite. "That's Danny."

Norman nodded. "We followed protocol. He changed, got dry, and we were out of there before the search teams could respond."

163

A silence settled between them, heavy but not uncomfortable. The kind that existed between people who had crossed a line they couldn't uncross.

Rebecca shifted slightly. "And your share?"

Norman didn't move. "Properly arranged."

That was all she needed to hear. It wasn't a question she was supposed to ask, and he had no intention of answering.

She let it go.

"What about you?" she asked instead. "You're done, right?"

Norman's smirk flickered, brief as the streetlights behind them. "I'm almost done. Just like you."

Rebecca studied him. "You don't seem convinced."

He let out a slow breath, stretching his legs in front of him. "I've done a lot of things in my career. Some questionable. Some straight-up dirty. But this?" He shook his head slightly. "This was different."

Rebecca scoffed. "Spare me the crisis of conscience, Norman. You knew exactly what this was when you agreed to it."

His eyes flicked to her, sharp. "Yeah. And so did you."

A tense beat.

Then Rebecca sighed, leaning back against the bench, mirroring his posture. "So, what now? You disappear?"

"Something like that," Norman muttered. He pulled another cigarette from his pocket but didn't light it. "Someplace quiet. Warm. Where no one asks questions."

Rebecca nodded as if that made perfect sense.

164

"You?" he asked.

A smirk tugged at the corner of her lips. "I have a plane to catch soon."

They sat in silence for another long moment, the tide rolling in, stealing more sand from under their feet.

Finally, Rebecca stood. "Well, Norman," she said, brushing a speck of sand from her sleeve, "this is it."

Norman nodded, but he didn't stand, didn't shake her hand. "Watch yourself, Rebecca."

She flashed a small, knowing smile. "Always."

And then she walked away, disappearing into the shadows beyond the boardwalk.

Norman sat there a little longer, watching the ocean swallow the footprints she left behind. Then he flicked his cigarette away, stood up, and walked in the opposite direction.

No looking back.

39. MR. PAIN

The night was thick with fog, rolling in from the coast and blanketing the city in a cold, suffocating silence. A single streetlamp flickered over a deserted industrial lot, its weak glow barely illuminating the cracked pavement. No cameras, no witnesses—just the kind of place where bad deals were made and worse things happened.

Norman sat in his car, gripping the steering wheel so tightly his knuckles turned white. His stomach churned, his nerves frayed. He checked his watch. 11:58 PM. Right on time.

A dark-colored car with muted headlights appeared through the mist, creeping forward like a predator stalking its prey. The black sedan came to a stop a few yards away, its engine still humming. The driver's door opened, and out stepped a man in dark clothes. This was the "Señor Duele" on the phone.

He moved with the casual ease of a man who had done this too many times to count. His leather jacket creaked as he rolled his shoulders, his cowboy boots scuffing against the pavement. He wasn't in a rush. He never was.

Norman exhaled sharply and grabbed the envelope from the passenger seat before stepping out of his car. The cold air bit at his skin.

Duele stood there, expressionless, a man completely at ease in the dark. Norman, on the other hand, felt like his skin was crawling. He hated this. He wasn't cut out for this.

But Danny needed this handled. And Norman needed Danny's money.

Duele smirked as Norman approached. "What do you want?" he said with a Spanish accent, his voice like gravel.

Norman swallowed. "You know what I want"

A long silence stretched between them. Norman cleared his throat, forcing himself to sound steady. "The job. It's urgent."

The mystery man tilted his head slightly. "Señor, this place gimme the creeps."

Norman nodded. "No cameras. No unwanted ears."

Duele smirked. "Smart." He pulled out a cigarette, lit it, and took a slow drag.

Norman clenched his jaw. Every second spent here made his skin itch. He lifted a manila envelope. I'll get straight to the point. Ten now. Another ten after, if you want." "All the details are in there."

Señor Duele took the envelope and grabbed two pieces of papers out without even paying attention. He looked at the information on the papers.

"I want this done clean," Norman said. "No mistakes. No loose ends."

Duele exhaled a cloud of smoke, amused. "Clean? Like an accident?"

Norman hesitated. "Untraceable. I'll leave that up to you."

Duele chuckled. "Claro."

Norman shifted uncomfortably. "Leslie is the priority. He first."

Duele nodded, unfazed. "And then the mujer?"

Norman hesitated for half a second. This part still unsettled him.

"She's extra, if you want the additional ten," he said, forcing his voice to stay even. "If we're cleaning house... might as well make sure nothing dusty is left."

Señor Duele studied Norman for a moment, then flicked his cigarette onto the ground, crushing it under his boot. "Cold-blooded."

Norman stiffened. Duele saying that felt ironic, considering his line of work.

"Do you care?" Norman asked, his voice quieter.

Duele smirked. "No. All the same to me."

Norman had no response to that. He checked his watch. This needed to be over.

"So?" he pressed. "Are we good?"

Duele gave him a slow, deliberate nod. "We good."

Norman exhaled, relief washing over him. He turned to leave, but Señor Duele's voice stopped him in his tracks.

"One thing."

Norman turned back, pulse spiking.

Duele's smirk widened slightly. "You sure you not on the list too?"

Norman stared at him. The words slithered under his skin like a toxin.

Señor Duele chuckled at Norman's silence and climbed back into his car. Norman stood there, frozen, as the black sedan disappeared into the fog.

For the first time, he wondered if he was handing out hits… or standing on the wrong side of one.

40. THE BARK THAT SAVED

The underground parking lot of Leslie's luxury apartment building was a cavernous space, brightly lit by fluorescent lights. Rows of sleek cars sat in silence, their metallic surfaces gleaming under the harsh glare of the lights. The air was heavy with the faint smell of oil and concrete.

Leslie pulled into his designated spot, the tires of his Mustang crunching softly over the smooth surface. He turned off the engine and sat for a moment, staring at the brown paper bag on the passenger seat filled with groceries. It was a mundane errand, but tonight, even the smallest tasks felt like a monumental effort.

He stepped out of the car and strolled over to the passenger side, his footsteps echoing faintly through the otherwise silent garage. He opened the door and grabbed the paper grocery bag out of the car.

The safety gate at the entrance rattled as it closed behind another car that had just entered, sealing off the outside world.

Unbeknownst to Leslie, Señor Duele had slipped through during that brief moment, his figure blending into the shadows.

Dressed in a delivery uniform with a logoed cap pulled low over his face, he moved with the quiet precision of a predator.

Duele crouched behind a concrete pillar, watching as Leslie moved toward the elevator at the far end of the lot. His target was alone, the isolation of the space providing the perfect opportunity. He slipped a small, silenced pistol from his jacket, the dull sheen of the weapon catching the bright light. This has to be the most daring assassination he's ever done.

Leslie approached the elevator, his mind preoccupied with thoughts of Lina and their crumbling plan. He pressed the button, the soft hum of the elevator descending breaking the silence.

Duele crept closer, each step calculated and silent. The distance between them shrank to mere feet.

Suddenly, a sharp bark pierced the stillness of the garage.

Leslie froze, his heart leaping into his throat. He turned his head instinctively toward the sound and locked eyes with a neighbor and her small, wiry terrier emerging from a nearby stairwell.

The barking startled Señor Duele, who flinched imperceptibly but enough to shift his aim. As he pulled the trigger, the bullet veered off course, ricocheting harmlessly against the concrete wall.

Leslie screamed, dropping his groceries and stumbling backward as he spotted Duele, gun in hand, just a few steps away.

"Help! Somebody help me!" Leslie yelled, his voice echoing through the empty space.

The dog's barking grew more frantic, the sharp yelps bouncing off the walls. Duele cursed under his breath, "Chinga!"

He fired at the dog a few times and nothing hit. The owner of the terrier got down and dragged the dog along with him. Señor Duele turned and shot at Leslie a few more times and nothing hit. Barking continued and it was a total mess and a huge distraction. It was unbelievable that a small dog could bark like that.

Realizing the mission was blown, Duele pulled his cap lower, concealing his face, and sprinted toward the safety gate.

Leslie scrambled to his feet, his hands trembling as he reached for his phone. His fingers fumbled with the screen, but his adrenaline-fueled panic rendered him unable to dial.

The dog owner, startled by the commotion, held the barking dog tightly, got up, and retreated toward the stairwell.

Duele reached the gate just as it began to descend after another car exited. He rolled under it with practiced agility, disappearing into the night.

Leslie collapsed against the nearest pillar, his chest heaving as he tried to catch his breath.

His mind raced, replaying the image of the man with the gun, the cold precision in his movements, the bullet that had narrowly missed him.

Someone had just tried to kill him.

Leslie stumbled into his apartment, his breath coming in ragged gasps. His hands shook as he fumbled to lock the door behind him. The underground parking lot felt like a distant nightmare, but the image of the man with the silenced gun still burned in his mind.

The thought repeated in his head like a broken record. Calling the police was the last thing on his mind. He grabbed his phone with trembling fingers and scrolled to Lina's number, pressing the call button. The dial tone rang once, twice, three times, but no answer.

"Come on, Lina," he muttered, pacing the room. "Pick up."

The voicemail clicked on, her sultry, automated message suddenly grating in his ears. He hung up and tried again. Still no answer.

Without wasting another second, Leslie grabbed his keys and bolted out the door.

41. CAT AND MOUSE

The mansion was eerily quiet, the soft hum of atmospheric lighting casting dim glows along the walls. On the nightstand in the master bedroom, Lina's phone ringed, Leslie's name flashing repeatedly on the screen. The faint sound of water rushing in the bathroom drowned out the ring tone, the steam creeping under the door as Lina hummed softly to herself in the shower.

Downstairs, the stillness was broken by the subtle scrape of a lock. Señor Duele, the failed assassin, worked the side door with practiced precision. The latch clicked, and he slipped inside, his dark figure blending seamlessly into the shadows.

The faint lights provided just enough illumination for Duele to navigate the hallway. He moved with deliberate silence, scanning the surroundings with a predator's focus.

He approached the staircase, his boots landing soundlessly on each carpeted step as he ascended. The faint glow from the master bedroom cast long shadows down the hallway, beckoning him like a signal.

Lina turned off the shower, wrapping a towel around herself. She wiped the fogged mirror, her reflection gradually emerging. For a moment, she gazed at herself, her mind racing with thoughts of the chaos in her life.

Her eyes flicked toward the slightly ajar bathroom door, sensing something. The hairs on her neck stood on end, but she shook her head and turned back to the mirror.

A crash shattered the silence.

Lina flinched, her heart racing. Outside, her cat bolted down the hallway, its tail puffed as it darted past a vase, sending it crashing to the floor.

The noise spurred Duele into action. Realizing his cover was blown, he rushed toward the master bedroom, gripping his gun tightly.

Lina's breath caught in her throat as the masked figure burst through the door. She screamed, slamming the bathroom door shut just as Duele reached it.

The doorknob jiggled. Then a moment of silence. Lina backed against the tiled wall, clutching the towel around her chest, her heart pounding.

Suddenly, the door splintered inward as Duele kicked it open. His silenced gun rose with precision, and he fired.

Lina dodged just as Duele fired, the bullet missed, striking the wall inches from her head. Lina screamed again, grabbing anything within reach—a soap dish, a shampoo bottle—and hurling it at the man.

Three more shots rang out, each closer than the last. One struck her arm, sending a searing pain through her. She stumbled, clutching her bleeding arm as Señor Duele closed in.

Just as he raised his gun to finish Lina off, a sickening thud echoed through the room. Duele dropped to his knees, the weapon slipping from his hand.

Leslie stood behind him, clutching a brick he'd grabbed from the landscaping outside. He stared wide-eyed at the masked man who now lay gasping on the floor.

"Leslie!" Lina yelled, her voice strained. "The gun! Grab the gun!"

Leslie froze, looking wildly around the room. "What gun?"

"The one under my mattress!" Lina shouted, using her good arm to point toward the bed.

Leslie bolted from the bathroom, skidding into the bedroom. Behind him, Duele groaned, in pain, struggling to his feet.

Duele, dazed but relentless, stumbled after Leslie. Lina gritted her teeth, grabbed the gun he had dropped, and fired. The shot went wide, shattering a picture frame on the wall.

"Missed!" Leslie yelled from the other room.

"No shit!" Lina barked, blood dripping from her arm as she hobbled after them.

"Where is it?!" Leslie shouted, frantically tossing pillows and blankets off the bed.

"My side!" Lina called from the hallway.

176

"Which side is your side?"

"The messy side, you idiot!"

Before Leslie could respond, Duele caught up, pulling a gleaming knife from his jacket.

"I finish you here," Duele snarled, lunging forward.

Lina appeared just in time, her aim steadier this time. She pulled the trigger despite in pain.

The shot, even though muffled, reverberated through the room, and Señor Duele dropped, clutching his side. He crumpled to the floor, his knife slipping from his grasp.

Leslie stared in shock, still holding a pillow. "Where's the gun?"

"There is no gun!" Lina snapped, lowering the weapon.

"What?! Then why'd you tell me to grab it?"

"Because he wouldn't have gone after you if I hadn't!"

Leslie dropped the pillow, his voice rising. "You could've killed me!"

"Well, I didn't, did I?" Lina shot back.

The tension broke into an uneasy silence as Lina kicked Duele, ensuring he was out cold. She gestured toward the knife.

"Grab it, Leslie! If he moves, stab him in the head."

Leslie gulped but obeyed, picking up the knife with trembling hands. Lina crouched down and pulled the mask off Duele.

She stared at the unfamiliar face, her expression a mix of exhaustion and disbelief.

"Who the hell is this?" she muttered under her breath.

42. AFTERMATH

The mansion was a war zone of flashing red and blue lights. The sound of police radios crackled in the night air, mixing with the murmured voices of officers processing the scene. The front lawn had turned into an impromptu command post—detectives, paramedics, and forensic techs moving like shadows under the glow of the streetlights.

Inside, Detective Martin Morales stood in the grand living room, his sharp eyes flickering between Lina and Leslie. The two of them sat on opposite ends of the couch, shaken but eerily quiet.

A few feet away, the lifeless body of Ramirez lay under a white sheet, a crimson stain soaking through where Lina had shot him. A forensics tech snapped photographs, the flash punctuating the tension in the room.

Morales glanced at the body before fixing his gaze on Lina. This was the second time he had crossed paths with her. The first was at the marina when Danny supposedly drowned. Now, just days later, she was standing over a dead man in her own home.

"Walk me through it." Morales' voice was calm, but his tone left no room for embellishment.

Lina swallowed hard, keeping her expression steady. "I was in the shower when I heard a noise. Next thing I knew, there was a masked man in my bedroom pointing a gun at me."

Morales turned to Leslie. "And you just happened to show up?"

"I tried calling her. She wasn't answering," Leslie said, rubbing his face. "So I drove over. The second I walked in, I saw him about to shoot her. I hit him with a brick, and we fought."

Morales tilted his head slightly. "Hell of a coincidence, don't you think?"

Neither of them responded.

Morales folded his arms. "Let me get this straight. First, your husband drowns in an accident where there's no body. And now, out of all the people in Los Angeles, someone breaks into your house and tries to kill you?" He let the words hang between them. "That doesn't smell like a robbery, Mrs. Carter. It smells like a hit."

Lina shifted uncomfortably. "I don't know what to tell you, Detective. I don't know who he is or why he came after me."

Morales stared at her, his eyes unreadable. "Sure you don't."

He nodded to one of his officers. "Get the prints off the body. Run them through the system."

Lina tensed. If Señor Duele had any prior records, Morales would soon know exactly who he was—and that would lead to more uncomfortable questions.

Morales leaned down, resting a hand on the back of the couch, his voice dropping.

"Here's what's gonna happen. Neither of you are leaving town. And tomorrow morning, you're both coming to the station for a full interview. I suggest you come clean about anything you might be holding back—because trust me, I will find it out anyway."

His gaze lingered on them for a second longer before stepping back. "We're done here. For now."

With that, Morales walked out, leaving them in silence as the police finished their work.

43. THE TRUTH REVEALED

Lina couldn't stay in that house another second.

The moment the last police cruiser pulled away, she grabbed her bag and told Leslie they needed to leave.

Leslie drove in silence, his hands gripping the wheel tightly. The streets of Los Angeles blurred past, neon signs and headlights streaking in the dark. The hum of the car engine was the only sound between them.

Lina's pulse pounded in her ears. Morales was putting pressure on them. The police would keep digging. The walls were closing in fast.

She exhaled shakily. "Leslie…"

He didn't respond, just kept driving.

She turned to him, her voice softer this time. "I have to tell you something."

Still, nothing.

Then, barely above a whisper—"This was all a scam."

Leslie's hands tightened around the steering wheel. "What?"

Lina took a deep breath, knowing there was no way to sugarcoat it. "Danny and I planned this. All of it. His disappearance. The insurance claim. The money." She swallowed hard. "You were just supposed to be the fall guy."

The tires screeched as Leslie slammed the brakes.

The Mustang jerked to a halt on the side of the road, the sudden motion jolting them forward. Leslie turned to face her, his eyes burning with disbelief and rage.

"I was what?" he said slowly, as if he hadn't heard her right.

Lina's throat went dry. "Danny—he… he made it look like you were involved. If anything went wrong, you'd take the fall. It wasn't supposed to—"

Leslie laughed bitterly, shaking his head. "Jesus Christ, Lina. I almost got killed tonight over this scam."

She reached for him, but he pulled away, pushing the door open.

"Leslie, wait—"

He stepped out of the car, running a hand through his hair, got on the sidewalk and paced back and forth. Lina lowered the window. Leslie let out a harsh breath before turning back to her, eyes hard.

"I don't want to see you again," he said. "I don't care what Morales does—I'm working with the police now. Even if it means I go to prison, at least I'll still be alive."

Lina just sat there, gripping the edge of the seat, her world crumbling around her.

Leslie came off from the sidewalk and marched back, stopped before the passenger side of the car. His voice was lower now, but the anger was still there.

"You want my advice? Show up and explain everything to the police. Then maybe, just maybe you can get out of this god damned mess in one piece."

Then, without another word, he turned and walked into the night, leaving Lina sitting in the passenger's seat of the Mustang she had bought him—alone.

44. A BURSTED PLAN

The villa overlooked a pristine coastline, its expansive terrace bathed in moonlight. Beyond the infinity pool, the waves crashed against jagged rocks, a soothing rhythm that contrasted with the storm brewing inside. Danny sat in a designer chair under a canopy, his laptop glowing on the marble table before him. A glass of expensive scotch sat untouched next to his phone.

On the screen, Norman's face flickered into view. His home office back in the States was dimly lit, cluttered with papers and files. Though composed, Norman's furrowed brow hinted at the weight of their conversation.

Danny leaned forward, his voice low but seething with anger.

"You're telling me your guy failed? Failed? Got killed? And now Leslie is still alive, and the pro is dead?"

Norman sighed, his tone even but tinged with irritation. "Yes, Danny. That's exactly what I'm telling you. Things don't always go according to plan, even with the best laid ones."

Danny's knuckles tightened on the edge of the table. He glanced toward the dark horizon, as if searching for answers in the void. "This is unacceptable! I paid you to handle this, Norman. Now we've got loose ends running all over the place, and one of them is Leslie!"

Norman's jaw clenched, and his voice dropped an octave.

"Listen to me, Danny. Duele wasn't some street thug. He was a professional, and this was supposed to be a clean job. But Leslie got extremely lucky."

Danny slammed his fist on the table, the sound echoing across the terrace. "Lucky? Lucky? I don't pay for luck, Norman. I pay for results. Leslie's alive, and now he will be a problem."

Norman leaned back in his chair, his calm cracking under Danny's accusations. "Leslie's not the problem you think he is. He's guilty, Danny. You think he's going to run to the cops? Unless he wants to do ten or twenty year in prison. Not a chance. He's neck-deep in this, just like us."

Danny's eyes narrowed, his voice icy. "And what makes you so sure of that?"

Norman adjusted his tie, his confidence returning. "Because Leslie's small-time. He's not a fighter; he's a runner. He knows if he goes to the police, he'll implicate himself and end up behind bars. He's got no leverage and no way out. He'll disappear on his own, just wait."

Danny scowled, his fury momentarily tempered by Norman's logic. "And Lina? What about her?"

Norman exhaled sharply, as though dismissing the thought.

185

"Lina's in no position to make moves. She's desperate, scared, and backed into a corner. She won't risk exposing herself. She's as guilty as Leslie, maybe more so. She'll do what she always does—cry, manipulate, and survive."

Danny sat back in his chair, swirling the untouched scotch in his hand. "You sound confident, Norman. Too confident. But let me tell you something: if Leslie or Lina so much as breathes in the wrong direction, this whole thing goes up in flames."

Norman's lips curled into a faint, humorless smile. "That's why we're not leaving anything to chance. Duele was a hiccup, but he's gone now. There's no one left to tie us to anything. No loose ends, Danny. Leslie and Lina are liabilities, but they're contained. This whole incident will scare them into retreat. And once the insurance payout clears, none of this will matter."

Danny raised an eyebrow, his suspicion palpable. "How much longer is that going to take? You've been stringing me along, Norman. I need that money yesterday."

Norman's face darkened, his tone sharp. "The investigation is wrapping up. The police are about to rule this an accident, just as planned. My report will back that conclusion. Once I submit it, the insurance company will release the funds. But if you keep pushing me, Danny, you're going to make mistakes. And mistakes are how we get caught. Remember, I have a big stake in this too."

Danny clenched his jaw, his grip tightening on the glass. He leaned forward, his eyes blazing. "You listen to me, Norman. If Leslie or Lina screws this up, you're going to handle it personally. No more mistakes, no more excuses. You got that?"

Norman nodded once, his expression unreadable. "Loud and clear."

Danny stared at the screen for a long moment, then leaned back, his gaze fixed on the distant horizon. "Good. Because if this blows up, it won't just be the cops you'll have to worry about."

Norman's smirk returned, faint but defiant. "I'll keep that in mind."

Danny cut the call, the laptop screen going dark. He sat in silence, the weight of their conversation settling over him. The gentle lapping of the waves below offered no solace, only a stark reminder of the isolation that came with betrayal and greed.

Back in his dim home office, Norman exhaled heavily, rubbing his temples. The screen before him was dark, but the echoes of Danny's threats lingered in his mind.

Reaching into his desk drawer, Norman pulled out a fresh glass and his best bottle of scotch. As he poured, his hands trembled slightly. Duele's failure had shaken him more than he let on, and Danny's relentless pressure only amplified the tension.

Taking a long sip, Norman muttered to himself. "Too many moving parts... too many variables."

He glanced at the nearly finished insurance report on his desk. It was critical to finalize it within days; any delays could lead to more scrutiny, and scrutiny was the enemy of their plan.

Staring at the swirling liquid in his glass, Norman allowed himself a brief moment of doubt. Then, he pushed it away, his mind sharpening.

"One more move," he whispered. "Just one more, and this nightmare is over."

But even as he said it, a faint unease settled in his chest. He'd cleaned up a lot of messes in his career, but this one was starting to feel different. It wasn't just the weight of the crimes— it was the people involved. Danny's recklessness, Lina's cunning, Leslie's unpredictability... it was a volatile mix, and he knew it.

Still, Norman pressed on. He had to. The payout wasn't just about money—it was about finishing what he'd started and walking away clean, no matter the cost.

45. AN UNEASY ALLIANCE

Detective Morales leaned back in his chair, fingers steepled under his chin, his sharp eyes locked on the man sitting across from him. Leslie's face was pale, his hands gripping the edge of the desk as if the weight of his guilt might drag him under. The fluorescent lights buzzed faintly, casting a sterile glow over the small interrogation room.

"You're sure about this?" Morales asked, his voice calm but laced with doubt.

Leslie nodded, swallowing hard. "I've got nothing left to lose, Detective. If I don't come clean now, I'm dead."

Morales raised an eyebrow, leaning forward. "And you think coming to me wipes the slate clean? You've been complicit in a murder scheme, insurance fraud, Mr. Lai. You don't just walk away from that."

Leslie's jaw tightened, a flicker of frustration breaking through his nerves. "I didn't know it was a scam until it was too late. They used me. Danny, Lina... they played me for a fool. I didn't kill anyone."

Morales studied him for a moment, his expression unreadable. Then, the door to the room creaked open. Leslie turned instinctively, and his stomach sank.

Lina stepped inside.

She was dressed impeccably, as always, her hair pulled back into a severe bun, her makeup flawless despite the turmoil etched on her face. Her gaze flicked briefly to Leslie before she turned to Morales, her expression a mixture of defiance and fear.

"Detective," she said, her voice cool but wavering ever so slightly, "I'm here to cooperate."

Leslie let out a bitter laugh, shaking his head. "Of course you are. Right on cue."

Lina's eyes snapped to him, narrowing. "Don't start with me, Leslie."

"I thought I said I never wanted to see your face again," Leslie shot back, his voice rising.

Morales raised a hand, silencing them both. "Enough. If you two want to avoid spending the rest of your lives in a cell—or worse—you're going to sit here and talk like adults. Got it?"

The tension between them crackled like static electricity, but neither said another word. Morales gestured for Lina to sit, and she took the chair beside Leslie, keeping her distance as though proximity alone might burn her.

Morales leaned forward, clasping his hands together. "Here's the deal. I'm willing to hear you both out, but I need the truth. No half-baked stories, no omissions. If you cooperate, maybe I can talk to the DA about leniency. But if I get the sense you're holding back..." He let the implication hang in the air.

Lina glanced at Leslie, her jaw tightening. "I'm not holding back. I have as much to lose as he does."

"More," Leslie muttered under his breath.

Lina ignored him, her voice steadying as she spoke to Morales. "Danny set everything up. The fake accident, the insurance scam, all of it. I didn't know he was planning to double-cross me until it was too late."

"You didn't know?" Leslie scoffed. "You were his wife! You were in on the whole thing from the start!"

"And I just told you he betrayed me too, you idiot!" Lina snapped, her composure cracking. "You think I wanted this? You think I wanted to be shot at and chased down like some criminal?"

"Maybe you should've thought about that before you dragged me into your mess!" Leslie shouted back, his voice trembling with anger.

"Enough!" Morales barked, his voice cutting through the argument like a whip. "I don't care who's more betrayed or more guilty. The fact is, you're both in this now. And unless you want Danny Carter to walk away scot-free, you're going to work together. Am I clear?!"

Leslie slumped back in his chair, running a hand through his hair. Lina crossed her arms, her lips pressed into a thin line.

Morales softened his tone slightly. "Listen, you're both in a bad spot. I get it. But Danny's the key here. If we can nail him, you both have a shot at redemption. Without your cooperation, we've got nothing."

The room fell silent, the weight of Morales's words pressing down on them. Finally, Lina spoke, her voice low.

"What do you need us to do?"

Morales nodded, satisfied. "First, I need everything you know about Danny's plan. Every detail, no matter how small. Then, we'll figure out how to use that to bring him down. But you have to trust me."

Leslie snorted, shaking his head. "Trust. That's rich."

Morales shot him a warning look. "You don't have much choice, Leslie Lai."

Lina glanced at Leslie, her expression unreadable. "Fine. I'll do it. But only because I want to see him pay for what he's done."

Leslie hesitated, then nodded reluctantly. "Yeah. Me too."

Morales stood, straightening his jacket. "Good. Now we have some common ground. Let's get to work."

As he left the room, Leslie and Lina sat in tense silence, the weight of their uneasy alliance settling over them like a shroud. For better or worse, they were in this together now. And there was no turning back.

46. THE TRAP IS SET

Detective Morales sat at his desk in the dimly lit precinct, the soft hum of activity around him providing a steady background noise. The weight of his recent conversation with Leslie and Lina lingered in his mind. He leaned back in his chair, his fingers tapping rhythmically against the receiver of his office phone as he contemplated his next move.

It was time to set the trap.

With a sharp exhale, he picked up the phone and dialed Norman's number. The line buzzed twice before a cool, professional voice answered.

"Norman Fields speaking."

"Norman, this is Detective Morales from the LAPD," Morales began, keeping his tone calm and matter-of-fact. "I wanted to update you on the Daniel Carter case."

There was a pause on the other end of the line, and Morales could almost hear Norman's mind whirring. "Detective," Norman said smoothly, "what can I do for you?"

"We've concluded our investigation into Mr. Carter's disappearance," Morales continued. "After extensive review, the department has determined that the incident was... an unfortunate accident."

Another brief pause. Then, Norman's voice came through, laced with polite interest but undercut by a faint, almost imperceptible note of relief. "That's good to hear. I know this has been a difficult time for Mrs. Carter and everyone involved."

"Yes," Morales agreed, leaning forward, his elbows resting on his desk.

"I figured you'd want to know since your investigation plays such a key role in the insurance process. With the police findings finalized, there shouldn't be any obstacles in your report."

Norman cleared his throat, the sound measured but betraying a hint of satisfaction. "I appreciate the update, Detective. It certainly makes my job easier knowing the matter has been resolved on your end."

"Of course," Morales said, letting a faint edge of reassurance creep into his voice. "We're just glad to close the case and give Mrs. Carter some closure. I assume you'll be wrapping up your investigation soon?"

"Very soon," Norman replied. "I'll be filing my report with the insurance company within the next couple days."

Morales nodded to himself, pleased with how smoothly the conversation was unfolding. He paused for a moment, then added,

"Before we wrap this up, I wanted to ask—have you heard about the attempts on Mrs. Carter and her... friend, Leslie?"

Norman's hand froze mid-reach for his coffee cup, but only for a fraction of a second. He recovered quickly, lifting the cup to his lips. "Attempts? I'm afraid I'm not following, Detective."

Morales leaned back in his chair, watching him closely. "Someone made a serious effort to eliminate both of them. Thankfully, neither was successful. But it's troubling, don't you think? They're both linked to your case, after all."

Norman set the cup down slowly, his face a mask of calm professionalism. "That's certainly concerning. But as you said, Detective, my investigation deals strictly with the insurance claim. Any unrelated incidents would fall under your jurisdiction, wouldn't they?"

Morales's lips curved into a faint smile. "Of course. Just thought it was worth mentioning. Sometimes these... 'unrelated incidents' turn out to be connected in the most unexpected ways."

Norman didn't miss the subtle dig, but he refused to let it show. He nodded curtly. "I'll make a note of it. Thank you for the heads-up, Detective."

Morales nodded, his sharp eyes never leaving Norman. "Always happy to help. Let me know if anything else comes up on your end."

"Of course, Detective. Have a good evening."

"You too," Morales said before hanging up.

Norman sat in his leather armchair, staring at the phone in his hand. The faint glow of his desk lamp illuminated the files spread out before him, including the finalized draft of his investigation report. He placed the phone down carefully, his mind racing.

The police had concluded their investigation as an accident. It was the green light he had been waiting for. Everything was falling into place.

But Morales's mention of the assassination attempts lingered in the back of his mind like an itch he couldn't scratch. Had the detective been fishing for a reaction? Or was this just a coincidence? Norman wasn't sure, but he knew one thing: the longer this dragged on, the riskier it became.

He picked up the folder containing the report and flipped through it one last time, his eyes scanning the carefully worded conclusions.

He had crafted it with precision, ensuring every detail aligned perfectly with the police findings. No loose ends, no room for suspicion.

"This is it," he muttered to himself, locking the briefcase.

Morales leaned back in his chair, his arms crossed as he stared at the small recorder on his desk. The conversation with Norman played back, the investigator's measured tone confirming what Morales already suspected: Norman believed he was in the clear.

Morales smirked, his eyes narrowing. He wouldn't move too soon. Norman's arrogance was his weakness, and Morales intended to exploit it.

He reached for his notebook and jotted a quick note: Keep surveillance on Fields. Monitor communications. Next phase: tracking the payout.

"Let's see how clean you really are, Norman," Morales murmured to himself.

The trap was set. Now, all he had to do was wait.

47. PAYOUT IMMINENT

The cemetery stretched over the rolling hills, a quiet sanctuary where the dead rested beneath neatly trimmed grass and polished stone.

From this vantage point, Los Angeles sprawled out in the distance, the skyline softened by a layer of midday smog. It was a beautiful day—too beautiful for the business being discussed.

Rebecca made her way up the winding gravel path, heels clicking softly against the earth. She didn't care for cemeteries. The finality of them, the weight of them. But today, she found the setting fitting—there was a certain poetry in meeting Norman here.

She stopped in front of a sleek black memorial plaque set against a simple stone slab. "In Loving Memory of Daniel Carter." No body, just a name. Just a lie.

She smirked, brushing an invisible speck of dust off the engraved letters. Loving memory, my ass.

Behind her, footsteps crunched over the gravel. She didn't turn around.

"You're late."

Norman came to a stop beside her, his leather briefcase in hand. He exhaled sharply, adjusting his tie. "Took the long way up. Didn't want to be followed."

Rebecca finally turned to face him. "Anyone ever tell you you're paranoid?"

"I'm alive. That means I'm careful."

Rebecca rolled her eyes, but her smirk lingered. "So? What's the word?"

Norman glanced at the engraved name behind her before finally meeting her gaze. "It's done."

She studied his face, waiting for elaboration.

"Morales ruled Danny's death an accident. Case closed."

Rebecca exhaled, her body visibly relaxing.

"The insurance payout is set." He paused, then added, "And you're the beneficiary."

Rebecca's expression stilled. She blinked.

"Come again?"

Norman didn't flinch. "Danny changed the policy before he disappeared. You are the sole beneficiary and trustee. Full control over the five million."

For a second, Rebecca couldn't tell if she was surprised or impressed. This must've been the surprise Danny was talking about the last time they spoke.

She let out a small, breathy laugh. "That sneaky son of a bitch."

"Gives you carte blanche," Norman added. "How it's handled, how it's distributed. It's all in your hands."

Rebecca placed a hand on her hip, eyes narrowing slightly as she processed the revelation. "And what's the timeline?"

"A week. Maybe less." Norman glanced around the empty cemetery, lowering his voice. "Once it's transferred, you'll need to act fast."

Rebecca tapped a finger against her lips. "I'll need a reason to disappear."

Norman smirked. "You've been playing the grieving widow at the firm. Use it."

She scoffed, but nodded. "A sabbatical, then. Grief has been overwhelming, blah blah blah. Disappear right after the money clears."

"Make it clean. No loose ends."

Rebecca's smirk faded slightly.

A light breeze rustled through the trees, the silence stretching between them. Then she asked, "And Danny?"

"I already updated him," Norman replied. "He's ready. Once the payout is in your account, you'll meet him. Just as planned. He'll give you instructions."

Rebecca nodded absently, her gaze drifting back toward Danny's empty grave.

"And Lina? Leslie?"

Norman's expression barely shifted. He waved a hand dismissively. "They're not a problem. They're guilty too. If get caught, they would be looking at years and years of prison time. They'll either keep their heads down or skip town. Either way, they're out of the picture."

Rebecca took one last look at Danny's false resting place, the corners of her lips curling into a small, knowing smile.

The pieces were falling into place. Or are they?

48. THE FEAR OF FALLING

The Montenegro skyline shimmered in the distance, golden reflections bouncing off the sea as the sun dipped toward the horizon.

From the balcony of his villa, Danny Carter swirled a glass of Scotch, watching the world below like a king surveying his empire.

It wasn't the wealth that satisfied him. Not really. It was the security—the knowledge that no one could take this from him.

He had built this life from nothing.

He leaned against the cool marble railing, the weight of the evening settling on his shoulders. In a few days, the final insurance transfer would go through, and he and Rebecca would vanish. A clean slate. Untouchable.

Then why did his stomach churn like he was standing at the edge of a cliff?

1992 – SOMEWHERE IN OHIO

The boy in the bunk below wouldn't stop crying.

Danny squeezed his eyes shut and pulled the thin, scratchy blanket over his head. The mattress reeked of mildew. The springs dug into his back.

Another whimper from the kid.

Danny turned over and muttered, "Shut up."

The boy kept sniffling, voice barely above a whisper. "I—I just want my mom."

Danny clenched his jaw. He wanted to say, *She ain't coming back.* But the truth was, he didn't know what had happened to her. Some kids got sent back home. Some disappeared. He had learned, early on, to stop asking.

The door creaked open. Heavy boots. The night shift caretaker of the orphanage.

Danny shut his eyes, feigning sleep.

He heard the boy get yanked from the bunk. A sharp cry. Then silence.

Danny didn't move. Didn't breathe. Just counted the seconds. *One, two, three, four...* He counted to a hundred. Then two hundred.

The boy never came back.

Danny's grip tightened around the glass. He exhaled slowly, placing it down on the railing before he shattered it.

Fear. That's what it was.

Not of getting caught. Not even of going to prison.

It was the fear of falling back into nothingness. Of being powerless. Of having someone else control his fate.

It's why he had studied harder than anyone in high school, clawed his way into college, learned everything about money, investments, loopholes. It's why he lied, manipulated, played people like chess pieces—because the world didn't give a damn about kids like him.

You took what you could. Or you got left behind.

That's what people like Leslie and Lina would never understand.

They thought he was greedy. Ruthless.

They didn't understand that survival wasn't greed. Survival was never letting anyone have power over you again. Danny closed his eyes and inhaled the ocean air. Soon, it would all be over.

One last transaction. One last move. Then, he'd disappear forever.

And this time, there'd be no one left to take it away from him.

49. THE EVIDENCE EXCHANGE

The office buzzed with its usual rhythm of ringing phones and the low hum of conversation. But in James's corner office, the atmosphere was tense and charged. Michael Langston sat across from James, a thick folder of documents spread out on the polished mahogany desk between them.

"This is it," Michael said, his voice low but firm. "Every missing dollar, every suspicious transfer, every breadcrumb we've managed to trace—it all points to Danny and Rebecca."

James leaned back in his chair, rubbing his temples. The past months had been a whirlwind of suspicion and revelations, but now the pieces of the puzzle were finally in place.

"You're absolutely sure about this?" James asked, his tone betraying the weight of the decision ahead.

Michael nodded. "It's all here. AI did a great job! Offshore accounts in shell company names, wire transfers routed through layers of obfuscation, even falsified client statements. Danny was the mastermind, but Rebecca... she wasn't just complicit. She was actively helping him cover his tracks."

James stared at the folder, his jaw tightening. "And the clients? How badly are they affected?"

Michael hesitated. "I have to tell you James, if this gets out, the firm's done, even if we make them whole."

James's face cringed, standing and pacing to the window. He gazed out at the city skyline, the weight of years of work and trust pressing down on him.

"This isn't just about the firm," he said, turning back to Michael. "It's about justice. Danny and Rebecca think they've outsmarted everyone, that they can walk away from this unscathed."

Michael folded his hands on the desk. "Then let's make sure they don't."

Detective Martin Morales flipped through the folder, his sharp eyes scanning the documents with practiced precision. James and Michael sat across from him, their expressions a mix of relief and lingering tension.

"This is good," Morales said finally, closing the folder with a decisive snap. "Really good. It corroborates everything Lina and Leslie have told us about Danny's activities—and then some."

James frowned, leaning forward. "So what happens now? Do you arrest Rebecca? Issue a warrant for Danny?"

Morales shook his head. "Not yet. The insurance payout hasn't been processed, and we want to catch them in the act. If we move too soon, they'll lawyer up, and tracking Danny in a non-extradition country becomes a legal quagmire."

Michael crossed his arms. "So what's the plan?"

Morales leaned back in his chair, his expression thoughtful. "We're letting the insurance claim proceed, but we're monitoring every step of the process. The moment the money lands in Rebecca's account, we'll have enough evidence to tie her to the fraud. As for Danny... we'll need her cooperation to bring him back."

James exchanged a glance with Michael, his brows furrowing. "You think Rebecca will turn on him?"

Morales smirked faintly. "Greed makes people do desperate things. And loyalty doesn't last long when people feel betrayed. We just need to apply the right pressure."

Michael nodded, but there was still a flicker of doubt in his expression. "And Lina and Leslie? Where do they fit into all of this?"

"They're cooperating fully," Morales said. "They've given us a lot of valuable intel. It doesn't excuse their involvement, but it's enough to make the D.A. consider leniency when the time comes."

James folded his hands, his voice heavy. "It's hard to believe Danny could do this. He was... a friend."

Morales's expression softened, but only slightly. "People aren't always who we think they are, Mr. Reid. Danny played a long game, and he played it well. But his mistakes are catching up to him."

He stood, offering his hand to James. "Thank you for bringing this to me. It's a crucial piece of the puzzle. Let's just play along with them for now."

James shook his hand, a grim determination in his eyes. "Let's make sure he doesn't get away with it."

As James and Michael left the precinct, Morales returned to his desk, opening the folder again. The weight of the case pressed down on him, but he allowed himself a faint smile. The net was closing, and soon, there would be no escape for Danny, Rebecca, or Norman.

50. REBECCA'S EXIT

The office hummed with its usual energy: phones ringing, the muted clicks of keyboards, and muffled conversations behind closed doors. But Rebecca Greene's footsteps down the carpeted hall carried a different weight. Her expression was carefully composed, but there was a faint tension around her eyes, a subtle tightness in her jaw.

She paused outside James Reid's office, inhaling deeply. This was the final step—one more performance before she could leave it all behind.

"Come in," James called after her light knock. Rebecca entered, clutching a manila folder to her chest. James looked up from his computer, his brow furrowed in concern.

"Rebecca," he said, gesturing to the chair opposite him. "What's on your mind?"

She gave a small, almost apologetic smile as she sat. "James, I need to talk to you about something important."

James leaned back in his chair, his expression softening with curiosity. "What's going on?"

Rebecca placed the folder on his desk but didn't open it. She folded her hands in her lap, exhaling softly.

"It's about my position here at the firm," she began. "I've been trying to push through everything, but... the truth is, I've been struggling. With everything that's happened—Danny's death, the fallout with our clients—it's become... overwhelming."

James's brow furrowed further, his eyes searching hers.

"Rebecca, I understand how hard this has been. It's been a difficult time for all of us. But you've been a pillar of strength through it all."

She shook her head, a faint quiver in her voice. "I've been holding it together for the firm, for our clients, but... I can't do it anymore. I need a break, James. A long one."

James's face fell slightly, the words catching him off guard. "You're... stepping away?"

Rebecca nodded, glancing down briefly. "I need to take a sabbatical. I don't know for how long, but I need time to process everything, to grieve properly."

James leaned forward, his elbows resting on the desk.

"Rebecca, I can't imagine how difficult this decision must be, but are you sure this is what you want? You've been such an integral part of this firm. I don't know how we'd manage without you."

Her smile was faint but resolute. "You'll manage, James. You always do. This firm is strong because of you and the team you've built. It'll survive without me for a while."

James sighed, rubbing the back of his neck. "If this is really what you need, I won't stand in your way. But I hope you know you'll always have a place here when you're ready to come back. You're still a partner here, you know."

"Thank you," Rebecca said softly, her voice tinged with genuine emotion.

She slid the folder across the desk. "I've put together everything you'll need to transition my accounts to other team members. I'll make sure the handover is as smooth as possible."

James picked up the folder, flipping it open to glance at the contents. His lips pressed into a thin line as he nodded. "I appreciate this, Rebecca. I really do."

She stood, smoothing her skirt. "I'll start preparing my departure immediately. I'll aim to have everything wrapped up by the end of the week."

James rose as well, extending a hand. "If there's anything you need during this time, anything at all, don't hesitate to reach out."

Rebecca took his hand, shaking it firmly. "Thank you, James. That means a lot."

As she walked out of his office, her steps were steady, but her heart raced. The first piece of her escape plan was now in place. All she needed was for the insurance payout to come through, and she could disappear from this life entirely.

She reached her own office, closing the door behind her. For a moment, she stood still, staring out the window at the city skyline.

A flicker of a smile crossed her lips.

Soon, she thought. Soon, I'll be free.

51. THE FINAL EXCHANGE

The waves crashed rhythmically against the shore, the tide creeping higher along the empty stretch of beach beneath the Santa Monica Pier. The neon lights from the Ferris wheel flickered in the distance, casting distorted reflections on the wet sand. A cool wind rolled in from the Pacific, carrying the scent of salt and the distant hum of city life.

Rebecca walked with purpose in her sneakers. She was dressed in casual wear. The ocean breeze had loosened a few strands of hair from her otherwise pristine appearance. She didn't fix them. This was the last meeting before everything changed.

Near a row of wooden pylons, Norman stood with his hands in the pockets of a weathered windbreaker, his stance relaxed, like a man with nowhere to be. He glanced up as she approached, his expression unreadable in the dim light.

"Rebecca," he greeted, nodding slightly.

She stopped a few feet away. "Norman."

There was no need for pleasantries. The air between them was heavy with finality.

Norman reached into his jacket, pulling out a phone. He tapped the screen once and turned it toward her—a banking confirmation. Five million transferred into the trust Danny had set up.

Rebecca studied the screen, her face betraying nothing. "Good." She let the word settle before tilting her head. "And your share?"

Norman slipped the phone back into his pocket. "Properly arranged." His tone was even, impassive. A clear signal—none of her business.

She didn't press. It was never about trust; it was about understanding the rules of the game.

The waves rolled in, retreating just as fast. The wind shifted slightly, carrying the distant laughter of a few late-night wanderers near the boardwalk.

Rebecca exhaled, adjusting the strap of her bag. "So… what about you?"

Norman smirked faintly, like he had been expecting the question. "Retirement."

Rebecca arched an eyebrow.

"No obligations, no surprises. Just… life."

She studied him for a beat. "Sounds nice."

Norman shrugged. "We'll see."

A silence stretched between them—not tense, not comfortable, just the natural conclusion to a deal long in the making.

Rebecca glanced toward the ocean, then back at him. "Well…
goodbye, Norman."

He nodded once. "Take care of yourself, Rebecca."

She gave him one last look before turning away, walking
back toward the boardwalk. The pier lights reflected in the
shallow water, distorted by the ripples of the tide.

Norman didn't watch her go. He simply turned in the
opposite direction and disappeared into the night.

No loose ends. No second chances.

Just the end of the line.

52. THE ARREST

The morning was crisp and quiet, the kind that made people linger a little longer in bed. But Norman, seated at his modest kitchen table, was already well into his second cup of coffee. His eyes scanned the news on his cell phone, his expression calm and collected.

He had always prided himself on his ability to stay one step ahead. The payout was complete, his share secured, and the loose ends tied up. Or so he thought.

A sharp knock at the door broke the silence.

Norman's head snapped up. He frowned, glancing at the clock. Visitors were a rarity, especially unannounced ones.

Setting down his mug, he rose and crossed to the door. Through the peephole, he saw Detective Morales, flanked by two uniformed officers.

Norman's stomach tightened, but his face remained impassive. He opened the door, leaning casually against the frame.

"Detective Morales," he said with a faint smirk. "To what do I owe the pleasure?"

Morales met his gaze with a steely determination. "Morning, Mr. Fields. Mind if we come in?"

Norman chuckled softly, stepping aside. "Not at all. Make yourselves at home."

The officers entered first, their eyes scanning the neatly kept space. Morales followed, his sharp gaze fixed on Norman.

Norman gestured toward the living room. "Coffee? Or are you here for something stronger?"

"Definitely something stronger," Morales said, his tone clipped. "We're here to ask you a few questions."

Norman folded his arms, his smirk widening. "Questions? About what?"

Morales didn't sit. Instead, he planted himself in the middle of the room, his posture rigid.

"About Danny Carter. About Rebecca Greene. About a five-million-dollar insurance payout."

Norman's expression didn't falter. "I'm not sure what you're implying, Detective. It was a tragic accident, by both of our reports."

Morales stepped closer, his voice low and firm. "You're a smart man, Norman. Smart enough to know when someone's bluffing. So let's skip the dance and get to the point."

Norman's smile faded slightly, but he remained composed. "Enlighten me."

Morales reached into his coat pocket, pulling out a manila folder. He tossed it onto the coffee table.

"Take a look," Morales said.

Norman hesitated before picking it up. Inside were photographs—grainy surveillance footage of Norman setting sail in a small motorized boat from a dock on the day of Danny's "accident."

Norman's jaw tightened.

"Recognize that boat?" Morales asked, his tone sharp.

"Because we traced its rental records back to you."

Norman glanced at the photos, his mind racing. But he said nothing.

Morales continued. "And then there's this."

He pulled out a second folder, containing financial statements. "A transfer of two million dollars to an offshore account in your name. Funny how that lines up perfectly with the insurance payout timeline."

Norman's composure began to crack, but he quickly masked it with a dry chuckle.

"Circumstantial at best," he said smoothly. "You're reaching, Morales."

Morales stepped even closer, his voice dropping to a near growl. "And what about Mr. Pain? The hitman you hired to clean up your mess. He's dead, but his burner phone isn't. We pulled the records, Norman. The texts, the calls—every single breadcrumb leads right back to you."

Norman's face hardened, his fingers tightening around the folder.

"You've got nothing," he said coldly. "No witness, no confession, and no proof that I was on that boat."

Morales smiled for the first time, a cold and calculated expression.

"We'll see about that," he admitted. "But I've got Lina Carter and Leslie Lai. They're talking, Norman. And they've got a hell of a lot to say about you and Danny."

Norman's confidence faltered, a flicker of doubt crossing his face.

Morales leaned in, his voice a deadly whisper. "You're cornered, Fields. You can play coy all you want, but it's over. You think Danny's gonna protect you? He's somewhere out there, probably living it up while you take the fall."

Norman set the folder down, his jaw clenched.

"You don't scare me," he said quietly, though the tremor in his voice betrayed him.

Morales straightened, signaling to the officers. "We'll see about that. Norman Fields, you're under arrest for conspiracy to commit fraud, obstruction of justice, and attempted murder."

The officers stepped forward, producing handcuffs. Norman didn't resist, but the fury in his eyes was unmistakable.

"You have this all wrong," Norman spat as they cuffed him.

"You can tell me how wrong I am back in the station," Morales said, his tone cold. "It's the beginning of the end for you."

"Get me my lawyer." Norman insisted.

"As you wish." Morales replied.

As the officers led Norman out, Morales remained behind, his gaze falling on the files left on the table.

Norman thought he was untouchable, but Morales knew better. The game was finally shifting in his favor. And he intended to see it through to the bitter end.

53. NORMAN'S GAMBLE

The small interrogation room exuded an oppressive cold, its stark fluorescent lighting casting harsh shadows on the gray walls.

Norman sat stiffly at the metal table, his usually confident demeanor replaced with visible tension. Across from him sat Detective Morales, his sharp eyes trained on Norman like a hawk sizing up its prey. Beside Norman, Claire Wells, his public defender, projected an air of calm authority, her steady presence the only thing keeping Norman from unraveling.

Scattered papers and files lay between them, fragments of a case that threatened to consume everyone involved.

Claire spoke first, her tone measured and professional.

"Detective Morales, after a thorough discussion with my client, he has come to understand the gravity of his situation. He's prepared to cooperate fully with your investigation in exchange for leniency."

Morales leaned back in his chair, his arms crossed over his chest, a skeptical smirk curling his lips. "Leniency, huh?" His gaze flicked to Norman. "You know, Claire, your client was singing a very different tune just a couple of days ago."

Norman shifted in his seat, his hands fidgeting in his lap.

"Look," he began, his voice edged with nervous energy, "I didn't kill anyone, alright? The hits on Leslie and Lina—they weren't personal. I was just following orders."

Morales's smirk faded, replaced by a hard, probing stare. "Orders from who?"

Norman hesitated, glancing at Claire for reassurance. She gave him a firm nod, and he took a deep breath.

"Danny Carter," Norman admitted. "He called the shots. Always did."

Morales leaned forward, resting his elbows on the table. His voice dropped to a razor-sharp edge. "Keep going."

Norman swallowed hard, the words tumbling out in a rush.

"I sold him that insurance policy years ago—back when he was attacked by a pissed-off client. It was just business at the time. But then... then he came to me with this scheme. He'd been planning it for years, faking his death, collecting the payout, disappearing. And he dragged me into it."

Morales's brow furrowed, his voice low. "Dragged you into it? Seems to me you were pretty eager to jump in."

Norman's frustration boiled over. "You don't understand! He offered me two million dollars! Two million!" He pounded the table for emphasis. "You think I could say no to that? Not at my age, not with retirement looming."

Claire interjected smoothly, her tone conciliatory. "Detective, Mr. Fields acknowledges the severity of his actions and is ready to provide critical information to aid your investigation. His cooperation will be invaluable."

Morales ignored her, his piercing gaze locked on Norman. "Where is he?"

Norman exhaled slowly, his voice trembling. "I don't know exactly. Danny's too careful to let me in on everything. But I did advise him to head to a non-extradition country. I think he knew that too. He's using a fake identity—one I helped him create."

Morales tapped his fingers on the table, his expression unreadable. "Who else is involved?"

"Rebecca Greene," Norman replied without hesitation. "She's his partner in all of this. She was handling the embezzlement while Danny orchestrated the rest."

Morales sat back, letting the confession settle like a heavy weight in the room. The silence stretched thin, the tension palpable.

Norman shifted nervously, his desperation bleeding through. "I've told you everything I know. Everything!"

Claire's voice remained calm and firm. "Detective Morales, my client's testimony has the potential to solidify your case against Danny Carter and Rebecca Greene. His cooperation will be instrumental in bringing them both to justice."

Morales stayed silent for a beat, his steely gaze never leaving Norman. Finally, he nodded, his voice hard and unyielding.

"Alright, Norman. But here's the deal: you give us everything. No holding back, no games. You step out of line even once, and that deal is gone. Clear?"

Norman nodded quickly, the relief almost visible in his posture. "Crystal."

Morales stood, gathering the scattered papers on the table.

"Good. Because the second you try to play me, you'll wish you never took that two million dollars."

As Morales left the room, Norman sagged in his chair, the weight of his decision pressing heavily on him. Claire placed a steady hand on his arm, but the look in her eyes was clear: there was no turning back now.

54. MOVING FORWARD

Detective Morales's office was dimly lit, the low hum of fluorescent lights buzzing faintly overhead. Lina and Leslie sat across from Morales, the tension between them almost as thick as the unease that hung in the air. Morales leaned forward, his fingers interlaced on the desk, his expression calm but calculating.

"Here's the plan," Morales began, his tone deliberate and firm. "Rebecca is the key. She's the only one who can lead us to Danny."

Lina furrowed her brows, her voice sharp. "You don't know where Danny is?"

Morales shook his head. "Not yet. He has probably fled to a country without an extradition treaty with the U.S.. But Rebecca won't stay here for long. With the insurance payout in her hands, she's going to skip town. That's why we're going to let her go."

Leslie's eyes widened, incredulous. "Let her go? Are you serious? She's going to walk right into Danny's arms!"

Morales's lips twitched into a faint smirk. "Exactly. And when she does, we'll be right behind her."

Lina leaned back in her chair, her arms crossed. "So, you're using her to get to him?"

Morales nodded. "Rebecca's the only person who knows where Danny is hiding. She's our ticket to finding him and bringing him back. But I can't do this alone."

He turned his sharp gaze to Lina and Leslie, his tone growing serious. "That's where you two come in."

Leslie's face twisted with uncertainty. "Us? You're putting this on us now?"

Morales leaned forward, his eyes narrowing. "This is part of the deal. You want leniency? You want a shot at immunity? This is how you earn it. You're going to follow Rebecca wherever she goes."

Lina blinked, taken aback. "You're asking us to trail her? Like some kind of spies?"

Morales's tone remained even, though there was an edge of urgency. "Not spies. Witnesses. You'll report her movements back to me. My team will handle the heavy lifting, but having you close will keep her off guard. She won't suspect a thing."

Leslie let out a bitter laugh, shaking his head. "This is insane. We don't know how to trail somebody. Isn't this FBI's job or something? What if she catches on? What if she realizes we're following her?"

Morales shrugged, his confidence unshaken. "Then you make it convincing. You play it cool. Rebecca doesn't see you two as a threat—she's too focused on her own escape. And if you stick to my instructions, she'll never see it coming. We will have the Fed's involvement too."

Lina exchanged a wary glance with Leslie, her voice low. "And what happens when we find Danny?"

Morales's gaze hardened. "Leave that to me. My team and I will handle Danny once we've got him. Your job is to get us there."

Leslie leaned back in his chair, running a hand through his hair. "So, we're just supposed to drop everything and become part of your operation?"

Morales's voice softened slightly, but his words carried weight. "This isn't just about redemption, Leslie. This is your chance to make things right. To bring down the people who used you, manipulated you, and almost killed you."

Lina's jaw tightened, her mind racing with the implications. She hated the idea of working with Leslie again, but she hated Danny and Rebecca more.

"And if we don't do this?" Leslie asked, his voice tinged with defiance.

Morales leaned back, his expression unreadable. "Then you're probably looking at 20 years. Both of you. And trust me, that's not a road you want to take."

Silence filled the room as Lina and Leslie weighed their options. Finally, Lina exhaled sharply, breaking the tension.

"Fine," she said, her voice steady but cold. "We'll do it."

Leslie hesitated, his frustration evident, but he nodded reluctantly. "Yeah... okay."

Morales's expression softened slightly, a glimmer of satisfaction in his eyes. "Good. My team will be in touch with your instructions. Stay alert, stay focused, and don't do anything stupid."

Lina and Leslie rose from their seats, the weight of their new roles pressing down on them. As they headed for the door, Morales called out to them.

"And one more thing," he said, his tone deadly serious. "This isn't just about Danny or Rebecca. This is about justice. Don't forget that."

The two exchanged a glance, the gravity of their mission settling over them like a storm cloud. For better or worse, they were in this together—and there was no turning back.

55. INSTRUCTIONS FOR ESCAPE

Rebecca sat alone in her home office, she did not turn any light on. The glow from her computer casting faint shadows on the walls. The room was silent except for the soft hum of the machine, a sound that somehow amplified her growing unease. She drummed her fingers on the desk, her eyes darting between the screen and her phone, which sat inches away.

The phone buzzed, shattering the quiet. Rebecca inhaled sharply, leaning forward. The notification flashed: "Secure line active."

She swiped the screen, connected her Bluetooth earpiece, and pressed the call button.

"I'm here," she said, her voice low. "Are you secure?"

A distorted voice crackled through the earpiece, calm and methodical. "Yes. You?"

Rebecca's gaze swept the room, her instincts on high alert. "Yes, secure."

"Okay," Danny continued, his tone all business. "First stop: Istanbul. I've booked you a business-class ticket under the alias that
Norman prepared for you weeks ago. You'll stay at the Çırağan Palace for two days."

Rebecca frowned, sitting up straighter in her chair. "Istanbul first stop? Why not just go straight to wherever you are?"

"This is to make sure you're not being followed," Danny explained, his voice clipped. "Pack light, you hear? You can buy everything you need here. When you arrive, lay low. No unnecessary calls, no emails, no contacts, no talking to people. Once you land, I'll be in touch, and we'll take it from there."

Rebecca's lips tightened. She ran a hand through her hair, exhaling through her nose. "This better work."

"It will," Danny replied firmly. "Stay sharp, do exactly what I say, and this will go off without a hitch."

Rebecca leaned back in her chair, her fingers drumming against the armrest. The tension in her body refused to dissipate, no matter how composed she appeared.

"I got it," she said after a moment, her voice tinged with resignation.

"Perfect," Danny said. "Talk later."

The line clicked. Silence filled the room again, but it was heavier now, pressing down on Rebecca like a weight. She stared at her reflection in the darkened window, the city lights twinkling faintly beyond. This was it. Her escape was in motion.

But could she trust Danny completely?

Her chest rose and fell in a deep sigh, her mind a whirl of doubts and half-formed fears. She reached for her glass of wine on the desk and took a long sip, as though the alcohol might dull the nagging unease that refused to let her rest.

A dark-colored minivan parked a few hundred feet away from Rebecca's driveway. The vehicle blended into the shadows of the quiet suburban street.

Inside, two figures sat in silence, their faces illuminated by the faint glow of a laptop screen. One of them adjusted the focus on a high-powered camera, its lens trained on Rebecca's home.

56. THE PURSUIT BEGINS

The sun cast a golden glow over the quiet suburban street as Rebecca stepped briskly out of her house, a sleek black carry-on rolling smoothly behind her. Dressed in a tailored jacket, oversized sunglasses, and a scarf that obscured part of her face, she moved with purpose. She paused at the edge of her driveway, her gaze sweeping the neighborhood with practiced subtlety.

Satisfied that she wasn't being watched, she continued to the curb just as a silver sedan pulled up. Without hesitation, Rebecca opened the back door, slid inside with her carry-on, and closed it gently behind her. The Uber driver gave her a polite nod before pulling away.

A block away, the dark-colored minivan that had been parked idly hummed to life. Its driver, an unassuming man with a calm demeanor, eased the vehicle into motion, trailing the Camry at a careful distance.

Detective Morales stood over a large table, a detailed map of Los Angeles and its surrounding areas spread out before him. An FBI agent, sharp-eyed and stoic, stood beside him, arms crossed.

Across the room, Lina and Leslie sat side by side. Lina cradled a coffee cup, her knuckles white against the ceramic, while Leslie tapped a pen nervously against his knee.

"This is it," Morales began, his tone carrying a mix of urgency and authority. "We're tracking Rebecca's every move. This is our best shot at finding Danny Carter. Once she's on the move, you two need to stay on her trail."

"No pressure, right?" Leslie muttered, the sarcasm poorly masking his unease.

Morales ignored the comment, his eyes fixed on the map.

"Exactly. No pressure. The second she realizes she's being followed, this operation collapses."

A sharp buzz interrupted the tension. Morales pulled out his phone, his expression shifting as he listened.

"Yeah?" he said into the receiver, his tone sharpening.

After a pause, he hung up and turned to the group with renewed urgency. "Showtime. Rebecca's heading to LAX. She's got a flight to catch."

The roar of helicopter blades filled the air as Morales led Lina and Leslie toward the waiting aircraft. The pilot, already seated and adjusting his headset, gave a brief nod.

"This'll get us to the airport ahead of her," Morales shouted over the noise. "We'll have eyes on her before she even checks in."

The trio climbed aboard, and within moments, the helicopter lifted off, the city sprawling out below them. Leslie gripped the edge of his seat, the aerial perspective doing little to ease his nerves, while Lina kept her gaze fixed on the horizon, her expression resolute.

Rebecca walked calmly into the bustling terminal, her carry-on trailing behind her. She approached the Turkish Airlines check-in counter, handing over her passport and ticket with an air of nonchalance.

Nearby, Morales' stakeout team sat inconspicuously among the travelers, their eyes following Rebecca's every move.

Morales, standing near a kiosk with his phone pressed to his ear, spoke rapidly into the receiver. After ending the call, he turned to Lina and Leslie.

"I just booked tickets for the two of you," he said. "Airport police will escort you through a restricted corridor so she doesn't spot you in the terminal. You'll be on the same flight."

Two uniformed officers approached, giving a brief nod before guiding Lina and Leslie toward a side door.

Rebecca, oblivious to the orchestrated trap forming around her, completed her check-in process and moved toward the security line.

Lina and Leslie settled into their seats at the very back of the plane. The cabin hummed with the quiet sounds of passengers stowing luggage and the occasional murmur of conversation.

Leslie fidgeted, glancing around nervously. "What if she spots us?"

"I doubt she booked a seat back here," Lina replied, her voice calm but firm. "Stay focused."

Moments later, Rebecca appeared in the aisle, her carry-on in tow. She scanned the cabin briefly before turning toward the business class section. Without a glance toward the back, she settled into her seat, adjusting her scarf with practiced elegance.

Unseen by her, Lina and Leslie exchanged a glance.

As the cabin lights dimmed and the plane taxied down the runway, Leslie exhaled deeply, gripping the armrest. "Here we go," he muttered under his breath.

Lina turned her gaze forward, her expression hardening. "It's only just beginning."

The engines roared, and the plane lifted into the air, leaving Los Angeles behind. For the first time, the players in this high-stakes game were all moving toward the same endgame.

57. THE RENDEZVOUS

Rebecca's journey began like clockwork, following Danny's meticulous instructions. Lina and Leslie, thrust into their high-stakes surveillance mission, two amateurs quickly realized how ill-equipped they were for such a daunting task. But for leniency, they would give it their best shot.

Back in Los Angeles, Detective Morales and his FBI counterparts provided them with a crash course on tailing techniques and how not to raise suspicion. It was like watching two laymen trying to mimic professionals in a game where one mistake could end the operation.

From Los Angeles to Istanbul.

The airlines flight to Istanbul was a long haul, but Rebecca sat in business class, perfectly poised, keeping her interaction with the cabin crew brief.

In the economy cabin, Lina and Leslie sat in the very back, tucked away and nervous.

Leslie leaned toward Lina, whispering, "You'd think for all the mess she's caused, she'd fly coach at least once."

"Focus," Lina hissed, adjusting her hoodie.

When the plane touched down in Istanbul, Rebecca disembarked calmly, her carry-on in hand. Lina and Leslie, got off the plane as fast as they could, trailed at a safe distance, blending in with the throngs of travelers bustling through the airport.

At baggage claim, Rebecca hailed a taxi and handed the driver a slip of paper. Lina and Leslie barely managed to grab their own cab before losing sight of her. They whispered hurried instructions to the driver, who seemed more concerned with avoiding Istanbul's chaotic traffic than their obvious panic. So far, things were going okay.

Rebecca's taxi pulled up to the Çırağan Palace Kempinski, a grand and luxurious hotel by the Bosphorus Strait. Lina and Leslie directed their driver to stop two blocks away.

"She's really pulling out all the stops," Leslie muttered as they watched her check in from afar.

For two nights, Rebecca remained a ghost. She rarely left the hotel, always keeping to herself. Lina and Leslie took turns staking out the lobby, nervously sipping coffee at the hotel café while trying to stay inconspicuous. They are exhausted.

Second Leg: Istanbul to Moldova.

Danny's next set of instructions came through Rebecca's encrypted line. She was to fly to Moldova next. Lina and Leslie, however, had no way of knowing this ahead of time.

When Rebecca checked out of the hotel and headed back to Istanbul's airport, Lina and Leslie followed as closely as they dared, careful not to get too close. From a distance, they saw Rebecca checking in.

"Which flight?" Lina whispered, her voice taut with stress.

Leslie squinted at the departure board. "There's only one flight to Moldova today."

"Perfect."

They rushed to the counter and purchased last-minute tickets. Lina asked for seats in the back, knowing it would keep them as far from Rebecca as possible. Luckily, there were some more seats available.

As they moved toward security, Leslie froze. "What if she spots us?"

"Then we're screwed," Lina replied bluntly.

At a duty-free shop, they hastily bought cheap hoodies and baseball caps to disguise themselves. During boarding, Rebecca glanced back briefly, and both Lina and Leslie instinctively turned away, hearts pounding. Somehow, they managed to slip past her gaze and board the flight undetected.

Moldova: Another Stop, Another Stakeout.

The plane touched down in Chisinau, Moldova, under gray skies. Rebecca moved with the same precision, taking a taxi to a boutique hotel. Lina and Leslie followed, keeping their distance.

"She's so predictable," Leslie grumbled.

"Predictable doesn't mean easy," Lina shot back, glancing over her shoulder.

For another two nights, the routine continued. Rebecca kept to herself, venturing out only for short walks and meals. Lina and Leslie, now slightly more confident in their roles, managed to stay close without raising suspicion. They did not know how many of these stops she was going to make. But they felt like it was close.

The Final Leg: Moldova to Montenegro.

Rebecca's third set of instructions from Danny came on the morning of her departure. She left her hotel and headed to the airport once again. But this time, Lina and Leslie faced a critical problem: there were two flights to Montenegro that day.

"What now?" Leslie asked, panic creeping into his voice.

They huddled in a corner of the terminal, hastily calling Morales back in Los Angeles.

"Split up," Morales instructed firmly. "You each take one flight. This way, we can't lose her."

Reluctantly, they followed orders. Lina and Leslie purchased separate tickets and parted ways at the gate, both praying they'd chosen the right flight.

Montenegro: The End of the Road.

Lina's flight landed first, but there was no sign of Rebecca. She waited in the terminal, scanning every face until Leslie's flight landed four hour later. Lina saw Rebecca come out of the exit. But she needed to wait for Leslie. But soon, Leslie hurried out of the exit as well.

"She was on my flight," Leslie said, breathless from running to meet her.

"I know, she's in front. Let's catch up"

Together, they hailed a cab and followed Rebecca to a secluded private residence nestled in the hills overlooking the Adriatic Sea.

The house was modern and pristine, its white walls gleaming under the sun. As they watched from a concealed spot, a familiar figure stepped out onto the balcony to greet Rebecca.

"Is that—" Leslie began, his voice trembling.

"It's him," Lina confirmed, her tone icy.

Danny had changed his appearance, as Morales had predicted. His hair was shorter, his beard neatly trimmed, and he wore casual, unassuming clothes. But there was no mistaking him.

Lina and Leslie sat in stunned silence, the weight of their week-long pursuit crashing down on them.

"We found him," Lina finally said, her voice a mix of exhaustion and triumph.

"Yeah," Leslie muttered. "Now what?"

Lina glanced at her phone. "We wait for Morales."

As the sun dipped below the horizon, the pair watched the house from a safe distance, knowing the trap was about to close.

58. BURYING THE HATCHET

The soft hum of the air conditioner filled the quiet hotel room as Lina sat cross-legged on the couch, a glass of wine in her hand. Across from her, Leslie slumped in an armchair, absently spinning a bottle of beer between his fingers. Outside, the evening breeze carried the faint sound of waves crashing against Montenegro's shores.

Neither of them spoke for a long while. The silence wasn't comfortable, but it wasn't tense either. It was simply the weight of everything that had happened, everything they'd done, bearing down on them.

Finally, Leslie broke the silence, his voice raw.

"I still don't get it," he said, staring at the bottle in his hands. "Why me, Lina? Out of all the people in the world you could've roped into this mess... why'd you pick me?"

Lina looked at him, her expression unreadable. She swirled her wine, watching the red liquid catch the dim light before taking a small sip. "It wasn't about you," she said quietly. "Not at first."

Leslie snorted, shaking his head. "Well, that's comforting."

"No, listen to me," Lina said, sitting forward, her voice firm. "You were... convenient. At the time, Danny and I needed someone—a fall guy, a scapegoat. Someone we could manipulate into doing what we needed."

Leslie's jaw tightened, but he didn't say anything. He just stared at her, his eyes hard.

"Danny came up with the idea," she continued, her voice softening. "But I knew it wouldn't work unless... unless I made it personal. You wouldn't help me if I didn't make you feel like you were saving me, like you were... important to me."

Leslie let out a bitter laugh, leaning back in his chair. "So you thought, 'Why not play the desperate damsel in distress and seduce the poor sucker into doing your dirty work?'"

Lina winced but didn't look away. "Yes," she admitted. "That's exactly what I did."

Her honesty caught Leslie off guard. He opened his mouth, but no words came out.

She took the opportunity to keep going."Do you think I'm proud of that?" she asked, her voice trembling slightly. "Do you think it was easy, pretending to feel something I didn't? But Danny—he... he made it clear that this was the only way to make the plan work. And I went along with it because I didn't think I had a choice."

Leslie's face darkened. "You always have a choice, Lina."

"Do I?" she shot back, her voice rising. "Do you know what it's like to be trapped in a marriage with a man who controls everything—every dollar, every decision, every aspect of your life?

Do you know what it's like to feel invisible? To know that no matter what you do, you'll never matter to him? Do you, Leslie?"

He stared at her, stunned into silence.

"I hated myself for what I did to you," Lina continued, her voice breaking. "But I didn't see another way out. Danny had all the power, all the money, and he... he convinced me this was our only chance to escape. He made me believe we could finally be free."

Leslie's grip on the beer bottle tightened, his knuckles white. "So it was all an act," he said quietly. "The flirting, the gifts, the... the nights we spent together. All of it."

Lina looked away, her eyes glistening. "At first, yes. But then..." She trailed off, her voice faltering.

"Then what?" Leslie pressed, his tone harsh.

She met his gaze, her expression raw and unguarded. "Then I started to care about you. And that scared me."

Leslie's breath hitched, and for a moment, neither of them spoke. The air between them felt heavy, charged with unspoken emotions.

"I don't expect you to forgive me," Lina said softly. "Hell, I don't even know if I deserve it. But I need you to know the truth. Everything I did—it was wrong, and I'll carry that guilt

243

for the rest of my life. But I'm not that person anymore. Not after everything we've been through."

Leslie leaned forward, resting his elbows on his knees. He studied her, his eyes searching hers for any sign of deceit. Finally, he let out a long sigh, running a hand through his hair.

"This whole thing's been one giant nightmare," he muttered. "But... I get it now. Why you did what you did."

Lina blinked, surprised. "You do?"

"Yeah," he said, nodding slowly. "Doesn't mean I like it, but... I get it. And honestly? I'm just as much to blame. I let myself get pulled into this mess because I wanted to believe I was doing something good. That I was helping someone who needed me."

He looked at her, a small, sad smile tugging at his lips. "Guess that makes me the fool, huh?"

"You're not a fool, Leslie," Lina said, her voice firm. "You're a good man who got caught up in something terrible because of me. And I'll never stop being sorry for that."

They sat in silence for a moment, the weight of their shared experiences hanging between them.

"So what now?" Leslie asked finally, his tone lighter, almost teasing. "We ride off into the sunset together?"

Lina chuckled, shaking her head. "No, Leslie. You and I—we're better off on our own. Too much history."

"Yeah," he agreed, smirking. "And too much drama."

They shared a laugh, the tension between them finally easing.

Lina stood, holding out her hand.

244

"Friends?" she asked, her voice hopeful.

Leslie looked at her hand for a moment before taking it. "Friends," he said.

As they shook hands, a sense of closure washed over them. Whatever had happened between them—whatever mistakes they'd made—it was finally behind them.

Lina smiled, pulling her hand away. "So, back to being a rideshare driver?"

Leslie grinned. "Maybe. But only if my passengers are as interesting as you."

She rolled her eyes, laughing as she grabbed her jacket. "Take care of yourself, Leslie."

"You too, Lina," he said, watching as she walked to the door. "And hey—try to stay out of trouble, alright?"

"No promises," she called over her shoulder, flashing him a mischievous smile before disappearing into the hallway.

Leslie leaned back in his chair, staring out the window at the Montenegro skyline. For the first time in what felt like forever, he felt... at peace.

59. PARADISE FOUND

Danny's luxurious Montenegrin villa was perched on a cliff side, overlooking the sparkling Adriatic Sea. The villa was a masterpiece of modern design, with clean white walls, expansive glass windows, and an infinity pool that seemed to blend seamlessly into the horizon. The sound of waves crashing against the rocks below provided a soothing soundtrack to the idyllic setting.

Rebecca stepped out onto the terrace, a silk robe draped loosely around her, the fabric catching the gentle breeze. She held a glass of champagne in one hand and gazed out at the setting sun. For the first time in months, she felt a weight lift from her chest.

Danny appeared behind her, wrapping his arms around her waist. He was dressed in casual linen pants and a button-up shirt left undone, a stark contrast to the sharp suits he used to wear. He pressed a kiss to her neck, and she leaned into him with a contented sigh.

"Do you believe it?" he murmured.

Rebecca smiled, tilting her head back to look at him. "Believe what?"

"That we actually pulled it off," he said, his tone tinged with disbelief. "No more looking over our shoulders. No more lies. Just us."

She turned in his arms, wrapping her own around his neck. "I'll drink to that."

They clinked their glasses, the crystalline sound ringing through the air. Danny leaned in, brushing his lips against hers. The kiss deepened, full of passion and relief, as if they were sealing their victory.

"Come on," he said, taking her hand and leading her back into the villa.

The interior was just as opulent as the exterior. The open-concept living space was filled with sleek, modern furniture, marble floors, and art pieces that spoke of wealth and taste. A gourmet dinner had been laid out on the dining table — fresh seafood, colorful salads, and a decadent chocolate mousse for dessert.

Danny pulled out a chair for Rebecca, and she sat down with a laugh.

"You're spoiling me."

"Get used to it," he said, pouring more champagne into her glass.

As they ate, they talked and laughed, their conversation flowing easily. Danny recounted the first time he had seen the villa, how he had immediately known it was the perfect hideaway.

Rebecca shared stories from her childhood, moments she had never felt comfortable sharing before.

"This place," she said, gesturing around them, "it's perfect. I could stay here forever."

Danny smirked. "That's the plan."

After dinner, they moved to the poolside. Rebecca dipped her toes into the water, the coolness a contrast to the warm evening air. Danny joined her, rolling up his pants and sitting beside her.

"You know," he said, his tone thoughtful, "we're free now. We could reinvent ourselves. New names, new lives. No one will ever find us."

Rebecca leaned her head against his shoulder. "I like the sound of that."

They sat in silence for a moment, watching the stars begin to appear in the sky. The world felt far away, and for the first time, they allowed themselves to believe that they had truly escaped.

Rebecca tilted her head up to look at him. "Do you ever think about what we left behind? The mess we made?"

Danny's expression darkened briefly, but he shook his head. "No point in looking back. We did what we had to do to survive. That's all that matters now."

She nodded, though a flicker of doubt crossed her face. She quickly buried it, focusing on the man beside her and the paradise they now called home.

Danny smiled, pulling her closer. "This is just the beginning, Rebecca. The world is ours now."

As the night deepened, they retreated back into the villa, their laughter echoing through the halls. They were two people who had gambled everything and believed they had won.

But unbeknownst to them, the trap was already closing in.

60. A DIPLOMATIC PUZZLE

The conference room at the FBI's Los Angeles field office was stark and utilitarian, its walls adorned with whiteboards covered in hastily scrawled notes and diagrams. Detective Morales sat at one end of the long table, flanked by a junior FBI agent, KAREN MITCHELL, and a State Department attorney, JONATHAN REESE.

Karen, a new agent in her early 30s with sharp eyes and a sharper tone, tapped her pen rhythmically against the table. Jonathan, dressed in a crisp navy suit that exuded professionalism, adjusted his glasses as he reviewed the dossier in front of him.

"Alright," Karen began, breaking the silence. "We've got Danny Carter and Rebecca Greene hiding out in Montenegro. We know their location, but thanks to Montenegro's non-extradition status with the U.S., getting them back is... tricky."

Morales leaned forward, his fingers steepled. "Tricky doesn't even begin to cover it. These two masterminded embezzlement, insurance fraud, attempted murder, and they're sitting pretty in a country that's giving us the cold shoulder."

Jonathan sighed, setting down the dossier. "Montenegro doesn't extradite its citizens or foreign nationals to countries with which it doesn't have a bilateral treaty. Unfortunately, the United States doesn't have such a treaty with them."

Karen frowned. "So, what are our options?"

Jonathan took a deep breath. "Option one: We rely on diplomacy. The State Department could pressure Montenegrin authorities to detain them on unrelated charges while we negotiate their surrender. But that could take months, even years, and we'd have to offer something significant in return."

"Option two?" Morales prompted.

Jonathan hesitated. "We could make a covert extraction attempt, but..."

Karen raised a hand, her expression hard. "No. That's a non-starter. Unauthorized operations on foreign soil are a legal and political nightmare. We'd risk damaging relations with Montenegro, not to mention the fallout if something goes wrong."

Morales rubbed his temples. "So, we're stuck playing the waiting game while these two enjoy their ill-gotten paradise?"

Karen exchanged a look with Jonathan. "Not necessarily," she said carefully.

Jonathan leaned forward, choosing his words with precision. "We've seen situations like this before. Sometimes, we can rely on local law enforcement to act in their own interest. If we provide Montenegro with sufficient evidence of Carter and Greene's crimes, they might detain them under their own laws."

"And then what?" Morales asked.

251

"We'd still need a way to bring them back," Karen admitted. "But if they're detained, it buys us time to figure out an angle."

Morales shook his head. "That's a long shot. Danny Carter's smart. If he catches wind of this, he'll disappear again. He's probably got backup plans on top of backup plans."

Jonathan folded his hands. "There is one more possibility. If we can convince Montenegro that harboring these criminals risks damaging their international reputation, they might cooperate informally. Countries without extradition treaties sometimes quietly deport individuals as a gesture of goodwill."

Karen arched an eyebrow. "Goodwill. That's optimistic."

Jonathan gave a half-smile. "Optimism is part of the job, Agent Mitchell."

Morales leaned back in his chair, exhaling deeply.

"Alright. Let's break this down. We need concrete evidence to present to the Montenegrin authorities. Karen, you and your team focus on compiling everything we've got — embezzlement, fraud, the whole nine yards. Jonathan, can you start laying the groundwork with the State Department? See if we can get any diplomatic traction?"

Both nodded.

"And what about Lina and Leslie?" Karen asked.

Morales's face hardened. "They're our wildcard. They've given us plenty already, but we might need them to go

252

further. If they can get something actionable while keeping eyes on Rebecca and Danny, that might tip the scales in our favor."

Jonathan adjusted his glasses again. "One more thing. If we can link any of Carter and Greene's crimes to international activity — offshore accounts, shell companies, anything — that gives us leverage to involve INTERPOL. It's a long shot, but it's worth exploring."

Karen nodded. "Understood, we'll dig deeper into the financials and see if there's anything that crosses borders."

Morales stood, his expression resolute. "We don't let these two walk away. Not after everything they've done."

The room fell silent, the gravity of the task before them settling like a weight on their shoulders.

Finally, Jonathan broke the silence. "We'll get them. It's just a matter of time."

Morales's jaw tightened. "Time is the one thing we can't waste."

61. A HIDDEN DETAIL

The dim fluorescent lighting of the detention center's visiting room cast a pale glow on the metal table and chairs bolted to the floor. Detective Morales entered the room, his expression hard and unreadable. Seated at the table was Norman, looking disheveled and tired, a far cry from the composed and sharp investigator he once projected himself to be.

Norman glanced up as Morales sat down across from him. His public defender, Claire, sat nearby, her legal pad resting on her lap. She nodded curtly at Morales, signaling that she was there to ensure no rights were violated, but otherwise, she remained silent.

Morales leaned forward, placing a small recorder on the table.

"Norman," he began, his tone clipped, "I know you've been cooperative, but I'm here to see if there's anything else you might want to share about Danny Carter and Rebecca Greene. Every piece of information counts right now."

Norman's eyes flickered with hesitation. He rubbed his hands together, his fingers twitching.

"I've told you everything already," he muttered.

Morales wasn't buying it. He fixed Norman with a steady gaze. "You've told me what I already suspected. But you've been in this game long enough to know there's always more. So, I'm asking you again—what else do you know about Danny's fraudulent activities? Or maybe some details you forgot to mention?"

Claire cleared her throat, her voice calm but firm.

"Detective, Mr. Fields has already provided substantial information. Let's not turn this into a fishing expedition."

Morales didn't look at her. His focus remained on Norman. "He has a chance to lessen the blow here. Cooperation goes a long way with the DA. But withholding information? That'll sink him."

Norman sighed heavily, slumping in his chair. The weight of his decisions seemed to press down on him all at once.

"Fine," he said finally. "There's one thing I didn't mention before."

Morales's brow arched. "I'm listening."

Norman glanced at Claire, who gave a small, approving nod.

"Danny didn't just plan his fake death," Norman admitted, his voice low and hesitant. "He also prepared for the aftermath. He knew that if everything went right, he and Rebecca would need to disappear for good. So, I helped them."

"Helped them how?" Morales pressed, his tone sharp.

Norman hesitated, but the look in Morales's eyes told him there was no point in holding back. "I connected them with someone who specializes in fake identities. New names, new IDs, new passports, everything they needed to start fresh. It wasn't cheap, but Danny had the money."

Morales leaned back slightly, digesting this revelation. "Who's this 'someone'? And how do we find them?"

Norman shook his head quickly. "I don't know his real name. Nobody does. He operates out of Eastern Europe, and his clients don't meet him directly. I only know him as 'Viktor.'"

"Viktor," Morales repeated, jotting the name down. "And you facilitated this connection?"

"Yes," Norman admitted, his voice barely above a whisper. "Danny trusted me to handle the logistics. Viktor provided everything they needed—passports, identification cards, even background stories. Danny and Rebecca have been traveling under those identities ever since."

Morales's jaw tightened. "Did you keep any records? Correspondence? Anything we can use to track this guy down?"

Norman shook his head again. "Are you kidding? Of course there's no paper trail. That's Viktor's rule. Everything was verbal, and the passports were hand-delivered through a courier."

Morales drummed his fingers on the table, frustration flickering in his eyes. But even as the obstacles mounted, he knew this was a significant lead.

"What else?" Morales asked. "Anything about the identities he gave them? Names, nationalities?"

Norman hesitated for a moment before replying, "Danny's using the name 'Nick Peters.' Rebecca's going by 'Anna Mozora.'

Morales nodded slowly, filing the information away. "This Viktor... how do I find him if I need to?"

"You don't," Norman said grimly. "Even I couldn't contact him directly. It's all layers of intermediaries and encrypted messages. Good luck catching him."

Morales leaned forward, his voice low and deliberate.

"Norman, you've just given me a lead I didn't have before. If this pans out, it could make a big difference for you. But if I find out you're holding anything else back..."

"I'm not," Norman said quickly, almost pleading. "I swear, that's everything."

Morales studied him for a long moment, then nodded and stood. He picked up the recorder, turning to Claire. "Make sure your client understands the stakes here. The DA will hear about his cooperation, but only if it's complete."

Claire gave a tight nod. "Understood."

As Morales exited the room, his mind was already racing. The fake identities, the passports, the name Viktor—it all pointed to a vast, shadowy network Danny had tapped into. Now it was a matter of connecting the dots before the trail went cold.

62. THE LEGAL LOOPHOLE

The conference room at FBI headquarters buzzed with energy as a team of agents reviewed maps, photographs, and documents pinned to a sprawling corkboard. In the center of the room, Detective Morales stood alongside Karen and Johnathan.

Morales leaned on the edge of the table, a fresh folder in hand. His expression was intense but controlled, the weight of the case etched into every line of his face.

"Alright," he began, addressing the room, "we've got new intel straight from Norman Fields. Danny Carter and Rebecca Greene are operating under false identities—Moldovan passports issued by a known black-market forger. Danny is now Nick Peters, and Rebecca is Anna Mozora. That means we've got leverage."

Johnathan, dressed in a crisp navy suit, leaned forward. "Leverage how, exactly?"

Morales met her gaze. "Entering Montenegro under fake passports is a clear violation of their immigration laws. If we inform their authorities through the embassy, we can get them picked up without needing to go through the usual channels for extradition."

Karen nodded thoughtfully. "It's a solid angle. We don't need to prove the insurance fraud or the embezzlement to involve Montenegro's local law enforcement. Immigration fraud is enough."

Johnathan crossed his arms, his sharp mind already working through the implications. "And once they're detained, what's the plan? Montenegro doesn't extradite to the United States, and they're unlikely to cooperate with a case of insurance fraud, even with strong evidence."

Morales smirked faintly. "We don't need them to extradite. We just need Danny and Rebecca detained long enough to make them sweat. They'll know the walls are closing in. That's when they'll slip up."

Johnathan tilted his head, skeptical. "You're counting on them panicking and making a mistake?"

"I'm counting on their arrogance," Morales replied. "Danny thinks he's untouchable. Rebecca thinks she's smarter than everyone else. People like that get careless when they feel the heat."

Karen tapped her pen on the table. "How do we involve the Montenegrin authorities without tipping our hand too much?"

Morales opened the folder, revealing copies of the fake passports and documentation Norman had described. "We give them this. Through the embassy, we inform them that these two individuals are using fraudulent documents to enter and remain in their country. That's enough for their immigration enforcement to act."

Johnathan flipped through the papers, his lips pressing into a thin line. "This... could work," he admitted. "But we need to tread carefully. If the Montenegrin authorities sense we're trying to manipulate them, they could stonewall us out of spite."

Morales nodded. "Agreed. That's why we keep it simple. We frame this as a courtesy notification—a heads-up about potential immigration violators. Let them take the lead from there."

Karen leaned back in her chair, her gaze shifting between Morales and Victoria. "Alright. Let's say we pull this off. What happens if they're detained? What's our endgame?"

Morales folded his arms, his voice steady. "Once they're in custody, we maintain surveillance through the embassy. We see how they react, who they contact, and whether they try to bribe or threaten their way out. If they panic, it could give us leverage to pressure them into cooperating—or at least give us insight into their next move."

Johnathan tapped his pen against her notebook, thinking. "We'll need to coordinate with the embassy carefully. If the local authorities act too quickly, it might spook them into running before we have a chance to intercept."

Morales shrugged. "That's why we make the notification now and let them handle the timing. Montenegrin law enforcement knows their country better than we do. They'll decide when and how to act."

Karen stood, signaling the end of the meeting. "Alright, Morales. Write up your report and I'll contact the embassy. Johnathan, you'll oversee the legal angle in case this gets messy."

Johnathan nodded, her expression firm. "Understood."

As the team began dispersing, Morales lingered at the table, staring at the photographs of Danny and Rebecca pinned to the corkboard. His jaw tightened, the weight of the case pressing on him.

"We're getting closer," he muttered under his breath. "One way or another, this ends soon."

63. LIVING THE GOOD LIFE

Montenegro's Adriatic coastline shimmered under the golden sunlight, its turquoise waters lapping gently against jagged cliffs. The cobblestone streets of the small seaside town were alive with the scent of freshly baked bread, grilled seafood, and salt carried in on the breeze.

Rebecca adjusted her sunhat, her bare shoulders glowing from the warm rays as she linked her arm through Danny's. They strolled through the bustling town square, where artists displayed paintings of the sea, and street performers strummed guitars.

"This place," Rebecca said with a contented sigh, "feels like it was plucked from a dream."

Danny smiled, his sunglasses reflecting the sunlight. "That's because it is. And now, it's ours."

They stopped at a quaint café overlooking the harbor. Rebecca leaned back in her chair, taking in the vibrant colors of fishing boats bobbing lazily in the water. A waiter arrived with two glasses of chilled white wine and a plate of oysters.

"To new beginnings," Danny said, lifting his glass.

Rebecca clinked hers against his. "To us."

They sipped their wine, letting the cool liquid calm their nerves. For the first time in months, they felt untouchable, as though the weight of their carefully constructed scheme had finally lifted.

After lunch, they wandered along the rocky shoreline, the sea spray cool against their sun-warmed skin. Danny kicked off his shoes, letting the waves lap at his feet.

Rebecca laughed as he splashed water at her. "Hey, watch it! This dress is silk!"

Danny grinned mischievously. "Maybe you should take it off, then."

Her eyes sparkled with playful defiance. "Not here, Mr. Carter."

They walked hand-in-hand to a secluded beach where the only sounds were the rustling of the palm trees and the distant calls of seagulls. Rebecca spread out a blanket, and they lay together, gazing at the endless expanse of blue sky.

"This is how it's supposed to be," Rebecca murmured, her head resting on Danny's chest. "Just you and me. No stress-free."

Danny's fingers trailed through her hair. "This is only the beginning, Rebecca. We've earned this."

As the sun dipped below the horizon, painting the sky in hues of orange and pink, they returned to the villa. The evening air was cool, and the scent of jasmine wafted through the open windows.

Danny had arranged for a private chef to prepare dinner. They dined on grilled sea bass, roasted vegetables, and creamy risotto. A bottle of vintage red wine stood half-empty between them as they lingered at the candlelit table, savoring each bite.

"This is what I imagined," Rebecca said softly, her eyes locked with Danny's. "Freedom. Beauty. You."

Danny reached across the table, taking her hand in his. "And this is only the start. I promise you, no one will ever find us."

Later, they stood on the balcony, the town's twinkling lights reflecting in the dark waters below. Rebecca leaned into Danny's arms, feeling the warmth of his embrace and the steady rhythm of his heartbeat.

For one perfect day, Montenegro had given them the illusion of paradise. But even in this moment of bliss, a faint shadow lingered—a reminder of the fragile foundation upon which their new life was built.

64. THE RECKONING

The Montenegro night draped the cliff side in a velvet shroud, the Adriatic Sea churning below with a restless, primal rhythm. The villa perched atop the rocks glowed like a jewel against the darkness, its white walls and glass panes reflecting the muted flicker of candlelight from within. Beyond the open terrace doors, the infinity pool shimmered, its edge bleeding into the horizon, a false promise of freedom. The air carried the tang of salt and the faint sweetness of jasmine, undercut by the distant hum of an approaching storm—or something far less natural.

Lina Carter crouched behind a low stone wall, her breath shallow, her dark trench coat blending into the shadows. The sneakers she wore—black, scuffed from months of running— pressed silently against the uneven ground, a far cry from the stilettos of her old life. Beside her, Leslie shifted uneasily, his hoodie pulled tight against the cool breeze, his hands flexing as if itching for something to grip. Below them, the villa's terrace framed Danny and Rebecca in a tableau of oblivious luxury— wine glasses glinting, laughter drifting on the wind.

Morales' voice crackled through their earpieces, sharp and clipped. "Surveillance feed's down—damn foliage or a signal drop, I don't know. Can't confirm they're still inside. Stay put, keep eyes on the villa. Police are ten minutes out. Do *not* engage, you hear me?"

Lina's grip tightened on the binoculars, the lenses fogging briefly from her breath. Through them, she saw Danny lean back in his chair, his linen shirt unbuttoned, a glass of red wine dangling lazily in his hand. Rebecca, in a silk robe, tossed her head back with a laugh, her fingers tracing the rim of her own glass. The sight twisted something deep in Lina's chest— anger, betrayal, a hunger for closure that had gnawed at her for months.

"Ten minutes is too long," she whispered, her voice steel wrapped in velvet.

Leslie's head snapped toward her, his brow furrowing beneath the hood. "Morales said stay put, Lina. We're not cops."

She lowered the binoculars, her eyes locking onto his— dark, fierce, unyielding. "He doesn't know Danny like I do. Five minutes, and he could slip away again. I'm not letting him disappear—not this time."

Leslie's jaw tightened, his gaze darting between her and the villa. "You're gonna get us killed. You know that, right?"

"Or save us," she shot back, rising to her feet. Her trench coat flared as she moved toward the winding path, her steps deliberate, driven by a fire that had been smoldering since

266

Danny's first lie. Leslie cursed under his breath, scrambling after her, his sneakers crunching softly on the gravel.

"Lina, wait—damn it!" he hissed, catching her arm. "What's the plan? We just walk in and say, 'Hey, surprise, you're screwed'?"

She shook him off, her voice low and fierce. "We keep them there. Distract them, stall them—whatever it takes until the police show up. You want him to pay for that hitman? This is how."

Leslie's eyes darkened at the mention of the hitman— Señor Duele's silenced pistol flashing in his memory, the barking dog that saved his life. He exhaled sharply, nodding despite the knot in his gut. "Fine. But if this goes south, I'm blaming you."

A ghost of a smirk crossed her lips. "Fair enough."

They descended the path, the villa looming larger with each step, its glass walls exposing every detail of Danny and Rebecca's evening. The terrace doors stood wide open, the breeze ruffling the sheer curtains, carrying the faint clink of glassware and Danny's low chuckle. Lina's pulse thrummed in her ears, a drumbeat urging her forward. Leslie matched her pace, his breath visible in the cool air, his hands shoved deep into his pockets to hide their trembling.

The front door was unlocked—a testament to Danny's arrogance, his belief that no one could touch him here. Lina pushed it open, the hinges creaking faintly, and stepped into the foyer. The scent hit her first—jasmine from the potted plants, the

267

rich aroma of grilled sea bass, the tang of spilled wine. The dining room opened before them, a scene of decadence frozen in time: the marble table strewn with plates, a half-empty bottle of vintage red, candles casting long shadows across the walls.

Danny's voice drifted from the terrace, mid-sentence— "Once we're settled, we'll move the funds to—" He stopped abruptly, his head snapping toward the sound of their footsteps on the polished floor. Rebecca froze, her wine glass halfway to her lips, her eyes widening as Lina stepped into the light.

"Hello, Danny," Lina said, her voice cutting through the silence like a blade.

Danny's glass slipped from his hand, shattering on the marble with a crash that echoed through the room. Shards skittered across the floor, wine pooling red like a wound.

Rebecca gasped, clutching her robe tighter, but Danny's shock morphed into a sneer, his dark eyes narrowing as he rose from his chair. He leaned back, swirling his wine, unfazed.

"Lina. You must be really desperate. Did you swim here?"

Leslie emerged from the shadows beside her, his face a mask of quiet fury, his voice low and steady. "All that running, all that planning… and you still couldn't see it coming, Danny."

Rebecca's breath hitched, her gaze darting between them. "What the hell is this? Danny—"

"Shut up," Danny snapped, his attention fixed on Lina. He took a step forward, his bare feet crunching glass, his posture coiled like a predator. "What do you think you're doing? You think you can waltz in here and what—ruin my night?"

Lina advanced, her sneakers silent on the marble, her trench coat swaying with each step. "Ruin your night? No, Danny. I'm here to ruin your life—like you ruined mine."

Rebecca stood, her voice trembling but defiant. "Get out! You have no right—"

"Sit down," Leslie barked, his eyes locked on Danny. "This isn't about you, Rebecca. It's him I want."

Danny's sneer faltered, a flicker of unease breaking through his bravado. He glanced toward the terrace, calculating an escape, but Lina stepped into his path, her stance unyielding. "Don't even think about it. The police are on their way. You're finished."

Rebecca's hands gripped the table, her knuckles white. "Police? Danny, what are they talking about?"

"I said shut up!" Danny roared, his composure cracking. His eyes darted around the room, landing on the dining table. In a flash, he lunged, snatching the serrated knife from the sea bass platter, its blade glinting in the candlelight. He brandished it at Lina, his hand steady despite the sweat beading on his brow. "Back off—both of you!"

Lina didn't flinch, her voice icy as she held his gaze. "You're not cutting your way out of this, Danny. Not this time."

Leslie stepped forward, hands raised, his voice calm but firm. "Drop it, Danny. You're not a killer—not yet. Don't make this worse."

269

Danny's grip tightened, the knife trembling slightly as his voice rose, raw and desperate. "You don't get it, do you? I've spent my whole life clawing out of nothing—nothing! I'm not going back to that, not for you, not for anyone!"

The distant wail of sirens pierced the night, growing louder, closer. Headlights flashed through the glass walls, red and blue strobing across the room. Rebecca backed toward the terrace, her voice a whisper. "Danny, stop..."

Lina's voice cut through, calm but venomous. "You're a coward, Danny. Always hiding—behind your lies, your money, your schemes. But it's over. Drop the knife."

Danny's eyes blazed with rage, his breath ragged. "You think you've won? You're nothing, Lina—just a pretty face I got tired of carrying!" He swung the knife wildly, the blade slicing the air inches from her.

Leslie moved on instinct, diving at Danny with a guttural shout. They crashed into the dining table, chairs toppling, plates shattering in a cacophony of porcelain and glass. The knife skittered across the marble, spinning out of reach as they grappled. Danny thrashed beneath Leslie, his fists pounding against Leslie's chest and somehow he flipped on top of Leslie.

"Stay down!" Danny growled, his breath hot and ragged.

Lina darted forward, grabbing a fallen chair and swinging it hard into Danny's back. The wood cracked against his spine, and he roared in pain, his struggles weakening. "You're done! You're done!" she shouted, her voice breaking with fury.

Rebecca screamed, stumbling back as the terrace doors burst open. Montenegrin police stormed in, their boots pounding the floor, weapons raised. "Ruke gore! Ne mrdaj!" the lead officer barked—Hands up! Don't move!—his voice a thunderclap in the chaos.

Leslie rolled away from Danny, panting, as two officers seized Danny, wrenching his arms behind his back and slamming him against the wall. Metal cuffs snapped shut with a harsh click, Danny's shouts—"You'll regret this!"—muffled by the clamor. Another officer grabbed Rebecca, who crumpled, sobbing, her silk robe tangling around her legs as they restrained her.

The lead officer switched to English, his tone cold. "Daniel Carter, Rebecca Greene—you're under arrest for illegal entry with false documents."

Lina stepped back, her chest heaving, glass crunching beneath her sneakers. Leslie rose beside her, wiping sweat from his brow, his torn hoodie hanging loose. Their eyes met—a silent, electric acknowledgment of their shared triumph.

Danny thrashed against the cuffs, his voice hoarse. "You don't know who you're messing with! I'll—"

"Save it," the officer snapped, shoving him toward the door. Rebecca's pleas trailed behind—"Please, this is a mistake!"—as they were dragged out, their silhouettes swallowed by the strobing lights.

The villa's serenity lay in ruins—shattered dishes, overturned furniture, wine staining the floor like blood. Police swarmed the room, barking orders in Montenegrin, rifling

271

through drawers and seizing the fake passports, euros spilling from Danny's luggage. The night air flooded in, sharp and cleansing, carrying the distant rumble of the sea.

Lina leaned against the wall, her hands trembling but her voice steady. "We did it, Leslie."

He nodded, a faint grin breaking through the exhaustion. "Yeah. We really did."

The officer gestured to them, his tone brusque. "You two—outside. Now."

They stepped into the night, the cliff side alive with police vehicles, their lights painting the scene in surreal hues. Danny's shouts faded as the vans pulled away, Rebecca's sobs a faint echo. The storm that had threatened the horizon held off, leaving only the stars and the endless sea to witness their victory.

65. LINA'S CLOSURE

The interrogation room was stark, its concrete walls stained a dull gray and its air heavy with the sterile smell of disinfectant. A single steel table sat bolted to the floor, its edges sharp and unforgiving under the harsh fluorescent lights. Danny Carter slouched in a metal chair, his hands cuffed in front of him, his face drawn but composed. His silence had been unbroken since they brought him in, and even now, as Detective Morales leaned across the table and laid out the weight of his crimes, he didn't flinch.

Morales stood tall, his voice calm but razor-sharp. "You're done, Danny. We've got everything. The offshore accounts, the fake identities, the insurance fraud—hell, even your little escape at sea. It's all tied up. You're going to prison. The only question is, for how long?"

Danny's lips were defiant. "You have nothing. You seem to forget that this is a non-extradition country."

Detective Morales smirked. "You really think you're smarter than everyone else, don't cha? You know, you could've gotten off scot-free, but you made one little mistake in all this tight planning."

Danny didn't say anything, but his face demanded for further explanation.

Detective Morales continued. "You should've entered the country with your real name instead of with a fake passport. Then, you could ditch your real identity once you're in. That goes with Rebecca too."

Danny's face changed from arrogance to realization. Detective Morales watched Danny's change of attitude.

"Now you're just being deported and we happen to be here to offer the both of you free tickets home on a FBI private jet just to make sure you're comfortable."

Danny's composure cracked. That was one little technicality he missed. But he swallowed his emotion.

Morales studied him for a moment longer, then straightened with a small sigh. "You know what? I think I'll give you some time to think about it. But you've got company waiting—one person who deserve some answers."

Danny's head snapped up, his eyes narrowing. "I don't have anything to say to anybody."

"Yeah, well," Morales replied, his tone sharp as he moved toward the door, "she's got plenty to say to you."

With that, Morales opened the door, nodding at the figure waiting just beyond. Lina stood in the doorway for a moment, letting her gaze settle on Danny. He looked smaller than she remembered, slouched in the metal chair, his hands cuffed in front of him. His clothes, once impeccable, were wrinkled and worn, and his hair was disheveled. For a man who had spent his life controlling everything and everyone around him, Danny now looked like someone who had lost all control.

Danny glanced up at her as the door clicked shut. For a moment, his expression was unreadable—neither cold nor welcoming, just blank.

"I guess Morales thinks this is my penance," he said dryly. "To sit here and listen to whatever you've come to say."

Lina didn't sit. She stayed standing, her arms crossed, her heels clicking softly against the concrete as she stepped closer to the table. "You owe me that much."

Danny smirked, leaning back slightly. "I don't owe you anything, Lina."

"Don't you?" she shot back, her voice sharp enough to cut. "After everything you've done, after everything you took from me—you don't think you owe me an explanation? Some kind of… truth?"

He scoffed, shaking his head. "The truth? Fine. You want the truth? Sit down, and I'll give it to you."

Lina hesitated, then pulled out the chair across from him and sat, her back straight and her eyes locked on his. For the first time in weeks, her composure wavered.

"Start talking."

Danny's fingers tapped lightly against the table, the cuffs clinking softly with the movement. He looked at her, really looked at her, and for a moment, something flickered in his expression—something almost like regret. But it vanished as quickly as it came.

"You were never the wife I wanted," he said bluntly. "Not really."

Lina's breath hitched, but she didn't flinch. "Go on."

"You were perfect on paper," Danny continued, his tone measured but biting. "Beautiful. Charming. The kind of woman people envied. You made me look good, Lina. That's why I married you. You were a trophy, a symbol. Proof that I was winning."

Her lips parted, but no words came out. The coldness in his voice felt like a slap, but she forced herself to stay calm, to let him finish.

"But you weren't enough," Danny said, leaning forward slightly, his eyes narrowing. "You never were. We had nothing in common, Lina. You didn't understand me, didn't understand what I wanted. You were content to live your little socialite life, posting pictures of our vacations, playing house while I worked to build something real. You had no ambition, no drive—nothing to offer beyond your looks."

"That's not fair," Lina snapped, her voice rising. "You don't think I tried? You don't think I gave up parts of myself to make you happy? I did everything I could to support you, Danny. I was there for you, even when you shut me out."

"Support me?" Danny laughed, a bitter, hollow sound. "You call spending my money and hosting dinner parties support? Don't kid yourself, Lina. You liked the lifestyle I gave you, but

276

you never cared about the work it took to get there. You didn't care about me."

Her hands curled into fists on the table. "And Rebecca did, is that it? She's so much better than me?"

"Yes." The word was a hammer, blunt and unforgiving. "She's everything you're not. She has brains, Lina. Talent. Drive. She doesn't just sit around waiting for life to hand her things—she takes what she wants."

Lina's jaw tightened, and her voice wavered as she spoke.

"You think that makes her better? You think that justifies everything you've done to me? To us?"

Danny shrugged, leaning back again. "It wasn't about justification. It was about survival. Rebecca understands me. She's my equal. With her, I didn't have to pretend. I didn't have to carry all the weight."

"And what about me?" Lina's voice cracked, but she pressed on, refusing to let him see how deeply his words cut. "You didn't just leave me, Danny. You destroyed me. You made me think there was something wrong with me, that I wasn't enough. Do you have any idea what that does to someone? To spend years loving someone who looks at you like you're a mistake?"

Danny's expression shifted for the first time, the faintest flicker of guilt passing over his face. He looked down at his hands, his fingers tightening into fists. "It wasn't supposed to end like this."

"No," Lina said, her voice steadying as she stood, placing her hands on the table. "It was supposed to end with you and Rebecca sailing off into the sunset, leaving me to pick up the pieces of a life you destroyed. You even hired someone to kill me! But guess what, Danny? You failed. And now you're here, and she's gone."

Danny didn't respond. He couldn't. For the first time, the weight of his choices seemed to settle on his shoulders, his cocky demeanor cracking under the pressure.

Lina stared at him for a long moment, her chest rising and falling with each breath. She had spent so many nights imagining this moment, wondering what she would say if she ever got the chance to confront him. But now that she was here, the words felt hollow. There was nothing she could say that would undo the damage, nothing that would make him see her the way she had wanted him to.

Finally, she straightened, her hands falling to her sides. "I hope Rebecca was worth it, Danny. I hope she was worth everything you threw away."

Danny looked up at her, his eyes tired, his voice quiet. "She was."

Lina felt a sharp pang in her chest, but she refused to let it show. She turned toward the door, pausing with her hand on the handle. Then she went back up to Danny and slapped his face in a solid manner. "I hope you rot in prison."

With that, she walked out, her heels echoing against the concrete as she left him behind. For the first time, she felt lighter, as if the weight she had been carrying for years had finally lifted.

Danny's voice, his lies, his betrayal—it no longer had power over her.

The door clicked shut, and Danny was alone.

66. DEPORTATION

The television screen flickered to life, the anchor's polished voice breaking through the ambient noise of the newsroom. Behind her, the faces of Danny Carter and Rebecca Greene were displayed, both wearing the expressions of defeat. The bright red chyron beneath them read: BREAKING NEWS: U.S. Fugitives Arrested in Montenegro.

"In a stunning development," the anchor announced, her tone a mix of gravity and satisfaction, "Daniel Carter, a former accountant accused of embezzling millions from his firm, and Rebecca Greene, a co-conspirator, have been arrested in Montenegro. Sources confirm the two were apprehended while traveling with false passports and deported back to the United States overnight. They now face numerous charges, including fraud, embezzlement, attempted murder, and conspiracy."

The screen transitioned to grainy footage of Danny and Rebecca being escorted off a plane by the FBI. Danny's face was hardened with anger, his jaw clenched, while Rebecca appeared utterly defeated, her head lowered and her shoulders hunched.

"The U.S. authorities worked closely with the Montenegrin government to ensure their deportation," the anchor continued. "They are faces serious charges back in the U.S. If convicted, they could face decades behind bars."

Detective Morales sat in the police department's conference room, his posture relaxed but his expression triumphant. Across from him, Lina and Leslie sat side by side, a mix of tension and anticipation hanging between them.

Morales flipped through a folder and leaned back, the barest hint of a smile on his lips.

"Well, it's official," Morales said, his voice steady. "Danny and Rebecca are back on U.S. soil. The district attorney and the FBI have reviewed your cooperation in this case, and I'm pleased to tell you both..." He paused for effect, savoring the moment. "No charges will be filed against you."

Lina let out a sharp exhale, as though she'd been holding her breath for months. Relief washed over her face, her shoulders visibly relaxing. Leslie, on the other hand, froze for a moment, disbelief etched across his features.

"Wait..." Leslie finally said, a small, disbelieving laugh escaping him. "You mean we're... free?"

Morales smirked. "Free to go. You've both more than earned it. Your cooperation was instrumental in making this happen."

Lina nodded, her voice quieter than usual. "Thank you, Detective."

Morales gave a small shrug. "Thank yourselves. And, uh…" His eyes twinkled with a mix of humor and sincerity. "Keep your noses clean, alright? I don't ever want to see you two again."

He stood and extended his hand. Lina and Leslie shook it in turn, gratitude evident in their eyes.

67. A BITTERSWEET GOODBYE

The city park was quiet at dusk, bathed in soft golden light as the sun dipped below the horizon. Shadows stretched across the manicured grass, and the gentle rustling of leaves in the breeze filled the air. Lina and Leslie sat on a wooden bench, both staring out at the tranquil scene before them.

For a moment, neither spoke. The weight of everything they had been through lingered between them, unspoken but palpable.

Lina broke the silence first, her voice soft. "It's strange, isn't it? Sitting here, just... breathing, after everything."

Leslie nodded, a faint smirk tugging at the corner of his lips.

"Yeah, it feels... surreal. A few months ago, I thought my life was over. Now, here I am, free, no handcuffs, no assassins trying to kill me. I don't even think this whole thing affected my credit score. Feels like I've been in some bad movie this whole time."

Lina chuckled, shaking her head. "You and me both. I never imagined it would end like this. I mean, I knew things would go bad eventually, but this…" She gestured vaguely at the park, at the quiet serenity around them. "This is better than I deserved."

Leslie turned to her, his expression softening. "Don't sell yourself short. You did the right thing in the end. We both did."

"Eventually," Lina muttered, her lips curving into a bittersweet smile.

They fell silent again, watching as a jogger passed by with a terrier dog trailing lazily behind. The orange and pink hues in the sky deepened, casting long shadows on the ground.

"You ever think about how it all started?" Leslie asked suddenly, his tone light but tinged with disbelief. "I mean, you got me into this because you… what? Saw me driving my sexy Prius and thought, 'There's a guy I can manipulate?'"

Lina laughed, genuinely this time. "It wasn't the Prius, I promise. You just seemed… different. Like someone who might actually care."

"Great," Leslie said dryly, though he smiled. "That's me—different and gullible. What a combo." Lina's laughter softened, and she turned to look at him.

"You weren't gullible, Leslie. You just have a good heart. Too good for someone like me."

He shook his head, brushing off the compliment with a wave of his hand. "Yeah, well, look where it got me."

They both laughed quietly, the tension easing.

"So," Lina said after a moment, leaning back against the bench, "what's next for you? Going back to being a driver?"

Leslie grinned, tilting his head. "Maybe. Why? You need a ride somewhere?"

Lina rolled her eyes. "No, I've got nowhere to go at this point. House got auctioned off. All the proceeds probably ended up in the hands of all the creditors. I still have some expensive bags I think I can get rid of. I'll find something to do."

Leslie nodded. He realized that they must go separate ways.

Lina continued. I'm good, I guess. Just... don't get infatuated with any female customers, okay? You're not great at picking the right women."

Leslie laughed, a full, genuine laugh that made his shoulders shake. "Oh, I'll try. Only with you, Lina. You're my one exception."

She smirked, but there was something softer in her eyes. "Well, you've got terrible taste."

"Clearly," he shot back, his grin lingering.

The light in the sky began to fade, the first stars starting to blink into view. Lina sighed, looking down at her hands.

"I guess this is it, huh?" she said, her voice quieter now. "The end of our strange little partnership."

Leslie nodded, his smile fading. "Yeah. It's time."

They both stood, facing each other awkwardly for a moment. Lina extended her hand, her expression steady but her eyes betraying a hint of emotion. "Take care of yourself, Leslie."

He shook her hand firmly, holding her gaze. "You too, Lina. And… thanks. For, you know, not getting me killed."

She laughed softly. "You're welcome."

As their hands fell apart, Lina turned and started to walk away. Leslie stood there and watched her as she moved on. He murmured to himself. "If she's interested, she'll glance back."

Lina kept on walking farther and farther away. Then, she stopped after some steps, glancing back at him.

"You really should go back to driving," she called out. "You never know who you might pick up."

Leslie grinned, his voice carrying across the growing darkness. "As long as it's not you again!"

They shared one last laugh, and then she turned and kept walking, her silhouette fading into the shadows of the park. Leslie watched her go until she disappeared from view.

With a deep breath, he turned and walked in the opposite direction, the quiet settling around him like a long-lost friend. For the first time in what felt like forever, the future was uncertain, but wide open.

68. IT'S FINALLY OVER

One Year Later – Miami

Lina stood behind the counter of her modest apartment kitchen, preparing a simple meal. Her phone buzzed on the counter. Detective Morales.

Lina's fingers hovered over the screen for a second before she picked up.

"Detective?"

"Lina," Morales greeted, his voice steady, familiar. "I thought you'd want to know—it's done."

Lina's breath caught. She gripped the phone a little tighter. "What did they get?"

"Danny, twenty-five years, no parole. Rebecca, fifteen. Norman… twelve, for cooperating."

A slow exhale escaped her lips, the weight of those words settling deep. It was finally over.

For the better part of the year, she had braced for something—an appeal, a technicality, an unexpected twist that would pull her back in. But there was nothing left to pull. The past had finally closed its doors.

"It's over," she whispered, as if saying it aloud made it real.

"It is," Morales affirmed. "And I wanted you to hear it from me. You and Leslie—once again, you both did well."

A small, knowing smile played at her lips. "Thanks, Detective."

Morales chuckled. "Just keep staying out of trouble, alright? I'd hate to see your name in another case file."

Lina laughed, a genuine sound, lighter than she'd felt in a long time. "No worries, Detective. I've been minding my business so far."

They said their goodbyes, and as Lina set the phone down, she gazed out at the street, bathed in the warm glow of sunset.

Las Vegas

Leslie pulled his car to the curb outside a diner. He was between rides when his phone rang. It's Detective Morales.

With a sigh, he answered. "Detective."

"Leslie," Morales said, his tone clipped but amicable. "Figured you'd want to know. Danny got twenty-five years, no parole. Rebecca, fifteen. Norman, twelve."

Leslie leaned back in his seat, a slow smirk forming. "About damn time."

"You're free of it now, Leslie," Morales said. "You can finally move on."

Leslie nodded to himself, letting the words sink in. "Yeah. It feels invigorating to hear."

There was a pause, then Morales added with a hint of humor, "And Leslie... stay on the straight and narrow."

Leslie snorted. "I'll try my best."

Hanging up, he tossed the phone onto the passenger seat and exhaled. It really was over.

Then, almost without thinking, he scrolled to Lina's name and hit call.

Lina picked up after the second ring.

"You heard?" Leslie asked.

"I heard," Lina said softly. "Morales called me too."

Silence stretched between them, but it wasn't awkward. It was full, charged with something unspoken.

"So," Leslie said, breaking it first. "How's Miami?"

Lina glanced around her small apartment. "It's alright. I work just enough to get by. Keeps me busy."

Leslie chuckled. "Same here. Vegas isn't too bad. You ever been?"

"A long time ago," she remembered.

"You should come check it out again. A lot have changed," he said casually, but there was something in his voice, something almost hopeful.

"I'm sure. And where might I find you?" Lina mused, swirling a loose thread on her sweater.

"Somewhere between Luxor and Stratosphere," Leslie smirked.

"I'll keep that in mind," she laughed.

"Well," he said, his voice lighter, teasing, "just don't let anyone steal your sweater pile, alright?"

Lina laughed, rolling her eyes. "Don't flirt with your passengers, Leslie."

A beat of silence. Then—

"Only with you."

Lina didn't reply right away. Instead, she let the words settle, let them mean something.

She glanced out at the city lights, at the possibilities beyond them.

"Good night, Leslie."

"Good night, Lina."

As she hung up, she stared at the phone for a moment longer before setting it aside.

Lina leaned against the railing, her gaze drifting upward to the stars. For the first time in what felt like forever, the future seemed wide open—and the past finally behind her.

EPILOGUE

The Las Vegas skyline shimmered against the desert night, neon lights flickering like electric veins running through the city.

From her suite at the Cosmopolitan, Lina Wilkins stared out over the Strip, watching the endless parade of tourists and dreamers, each one chasing something—a thrill, a fortune, an escape. She knew the feeling all too well.

She turned back toward the manila envelope sitting on the room desk. The weight of it was more than just the six-hundred-thousand-dollar check inside. It was justice, retribution, irony, and pleasant surprise all wrapped into one.

Six months after Danny's sentencing, the accounting firm had won its legal battle over what was left of his estate. And in the end, after all the creditors had devoured their share, Lina was the last one standing.

She picked up the check, running her fingers over the bank logo. It was more money than she ever thought she'd see again. But it wasn't just the amount—it was what it meant. For the first time in her life, she was free. No lies, no games. Just her and the future she was about to write for herself.

Lina hadn't told Leslie she was coming. She'd packed her bags, booked a flight, and checked into the Cosmopolitan on a whim, as if fate might handle the rest. Every night for three nights, she called for an Uber, hoping, just maybe, he'd be the one to pull up.

Every night, it was someone else.

She had treated herself to dinner at the Wynn, a quiet celebration for a victory only she understood. And now, standing outside the golden-lit entrance, she pulled up the Uber app ready to go back to her hotel at the Cosmo.

She entered the ride request. Momentarily, white Toyota Prius. Arriving in 3 minutes.

Her heart thudded as she saw the driver's name.

Leslie.

For a moment, she froze, her thumb hovering over the cancel button. What if this was a mistake? What if she got in that car and realized she had nothing left to say?

Then the familiar car pulled up to the curb.

Lina exhaled slowly. No turning back now.

Leslie had driven thousands of people in this city. He'd seen quite a few—high rollers on winning streaks, heartbroken drunks, and tired casino workers just trying to get home. But tonight, when he saw the name pop up on his screen, his stomach dropped.

Lina.

For a second, he thought it was some kind of glitch or perhaps a person with the same name. Then, as his car rolled up to the Wynn's entrance, he saw her standing there. Same piercing eyes, same effortless elegance—even in casual clothes, she looked like she belonged in another world.

She stepped forward, opened the front passenger door.

Leslie shook his head, letting out a disbelieving laugh. "Of all the Uber rides in all of Vegas…"

Lina slid into the seat, her smirk playing at the corners of her lips. "She gets into yours."

He stared at her for a beat, then shook his head again, shifting the car into drive. "You always did have a flair for the dramatic."

She exhaled, glancing out the window as they merged onto the Strip. "Yeah… guess I do."

A beat of silence settled between them. Not awkward, not tense. Just full of things unsaid.

Leslie finally glanced over. "So, as the Chinese say, what wind blew you to Vegas? Don't tell me you came just to test your luck at the slots."

Lina let out a small laugh, then reached into her bag. "Actually… I came to show you something."

She pulled out a check from her purse. A bargain purse. She holds up the check.

Leslie glanced at it at a red light, his jaw tightening as his eyes scanned the amount.

"Whoa," he muttered. "Six hundred thousand?"

She nodded. "Poetic justice, don't you think?"

He let out a low whistle, drumming his fingers on the wheel. "Danny must be losing his mind in that cell."

She smirked. "Let's hope so."

The light turned green, and Leslie drove in silence for a moment, the weight of everything settling between them.

Then, finally, he exhaled. "So... what's next?"

Lina turned her head toward him, studying his profile—the same man she had deceived, manipulated, been intimate with, fought off an assassin with, and, in some strange, unexpected way, grown to admire, love, and respect.

She didn't have an answer. Not yet. Instead, she leaned back in her seat, watching the street lights blur past. "I don't know," she admitted. "But I think I'd rather not figure it out alone."

Leslie smirked, keeping his eyes on the road. "That's a funny way of saying you missed me."

Lina arched an eyebrow. "Don't push your luck, Mr. Lai."

He laughed, shaking his head. "Too late."

The city stretched out before them, an open road leading anywhere. For the first time, neither of them was running.

Neither was lying.

As Leslie drove them toward the hopeful unknown, the past finally stayed behind.

THE 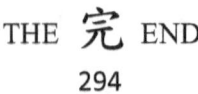 END

Acknowledgements

The idea for this novel first sparked during the fall of 2024, in a series of lighthearted chats with friends that unexpectedly led me down a darker, more thrilling creative path. I want to thank Leslie, David, and Phoebe for the laughter, the stories, and—yes—the unexpected inspiration born from our discussions on the curious complexities of double indemnity life insurance. What began as a joke in a chat group evolved into the crime-noir novel you now hold in your hands.

This is my debut novel, and like any first endeavor, it came with moments of doubt, many rewrites, and discovery. I hope readers find it engaging, cinematic, and full of the twists and turns that make storytelling such a powerful art form. I have many more stories waiting to be told, and I hope this is only the beginning.

A special thanks to Annie, my long-time friend, my beta reader, whose sharp eye caught many typos I tried to sneak past, and her encouragement meant more than she knows.

Last but not least, my sincere gratitude goes to Hollywood heavyweight Stratton Leopold (Executive Producer, *Mission Impossible III, The Sum of All Fears, Parker*), Dax Phelan (Director, *Jasmine*), and Eric M. Klein (Producer) for their belief in this story. Their generous testimonials helped give this book its wings.

Thank you to every reader who takes a chance on a new voice. "Angel with a Dirty Face" was written with the heart of noir, but it carries pieces of everyone who touched it along the way.

— James Su

James Su is a Hollywood-based independent film producer, screenwriter, and now, author—bringing his cinematic storytelling to the page. With nearly 30 years in the entertainment industry, he has worked on films that blend gritty realism, psychological depth, and visual artistry, crafting stories that stay with audiences long after the credits roll.

As a producer, Su has been involved in critically acclaimed films such as *She's Lost Control, Jasmine, The Other Side of the Wind, and About Him and Her*—all available on Amazon and Netflix.

His films have premiered at top-tier festivals including Berlin, Venice, SXSW, Telluride, Savannah, Mumbi, Stockholm, Vancouver, Vladivostok, Hong Kong, Karlovy Vary, and many others, earning international recognition. *She's Lost Control* was also nominated for Best First Feature at the 30th Independent Spirit Awards, cementing his place in the world of independent cinema.

When he's not writing or producing, Su continues to explore the art of storytelling—whether on film, on the page, or somewhere in between.

www.ingramcontent.com/pod-product-compliance
Lightning Source LLC
Chambersburg PA
CBHW021927240626
47158CB00002B/3